THE TELOMERE CONSPIRACY

THE TELOMERE CONSPIRACY

A DARK TALE FOR A NEW DARK AGE

BRUCE MASON

"You don't *like* how our world is going to end? Then show me another way—and please, no *deus ex machina* fairy tale ending," said Lou.

*Warning! Parts of this story are very dark and disturbing. Please do not read while under the influence of alcohol or drugs; exercise caution before operating a motor vehicle or heavy equipment.

iUniverse, Inc.
Bloomington

The Telomere Conspiracy
A Dark Tale for a New Dark Age

This book is a work of fiction. Names, characters, businesses, organizations, places and events are either the product of the author's imagination or are used fictitiously. Any resemblance to actual persons living or dead, events, or locales is purely coincidental.

iUniverse books may be ordered through booksellers or by contacting:

iUniverse
1663 Liberty Drive
Bloomington, IN 47403
www.iuniverse.com
1-800-Authors (1-800-288-4677)

Author contact:

thetelomereconspiracy@gmail.com

ISBN: 978-1-4620-5429-9 (sc)
ISBN: 978-1-4620-5430-5 (ebk)

Printed in the United States of America

iUniverse rev. date: 09/20/2011

CHAPTER 1

The near future, somewhere in America

"The world is mad and we're all going to die," said Lou, taking a large gulp of his ginger ale in Antonio's Bar. His old colleagues Tanya and Joe had invited Lou out for a drink, in a futile attempt to cheer him up.

"Come on Lou, is not bad like all that, *da*?" said Tanya, twirling a swizzle stick in her double vodka over ice.

"You're quite right, quite right, not that bad. It is, in reality, a lot worse." Lou turned his glum mug to the usually effervescent Antonio at the bar. Antonio's face fizzled to match Lou's doleful expression.

"Think back a few years. Remember the last big recession?" Lou continued. "The economy was so bad you would have thought the sky was falling. But back then all we had to worry about was money. The dollar was down, unemployment was the worst since the great depression, and the stock market was in palliative care. The only good investments were canned sardines and machine guns. The best-selling book was a do-it-yourself suicide manual."

"Hey, Luigi Gubriace," said Antonio, using Lou's full Italian name, "*Si*, it was a-bad a few years back but now things, they much better, eh? Now prosperity, she's just around-a the corner. Let a smile be your umbrella." Antonio opened his arms wide and gave Lou a smile as wide as a beach umbrella. Lou merely stared.

"And try not live up to old nickname, *Lou Gubrious*," said Tanya with a teasing smile.

Lou ignored the use of his detested moniker. "Now we can say what the heck, it's only money. Now we can forget about the economy and worry about whether life on earth will continue or die out entirely."

Tanya whispered to Joe, "Please to fasten seat belts, here we going again."

"I know, you think it's the same old rant. I'll talk about greenhouse gases, pollution, desertification, deforestation, ocean acidification, species extinction, permafrost melting in the Arctic, and aquifer depletion in the Punjab."

"Punjab? We haven't heard that one yet," said Joe. Tanya gave Joe a little karate chop in the ribs, and smiled a saccharine smile at Lou.

"Water shortages are severe in northern India, so the authorities drill more wells, deeper and deeper, and deplete the fossil water faster. But for Tanya's sake I'll spare you the details this time."

Antonio picked up the remote control and clicked the bar TV on. "Here's some nice pictures, take you mind off-a things, eh? Look at polar bear, Luigi, he's a-beautiful, and all that nice-a clean water, *mmm.*"

"Hmm. Not an ice floe in sight. I think the bear's treading water, contemplating his next move."

Joe grabbed the remote and changed channels. An image of an overcrowded shanty town in Brazil came on the screen, with thousands of impoverished people living in squalor. "There, I've seen that story on the news. They're going to move all those people into nice new apartments in the suburbs. Great, eh?"

"Suburbs. Right. More farmland paved over, so they need to have more rainforests clear-cut and burned to create more farmland, and so on in an endless cycle. Or until we run out of land to pave over."

Tanya tried her luck with the remote. She quickly skipped the videos of East African wars over arable land and water, gang warfare slayings in Mexico, economic protest marches in Greece and Italy, and finally settled on some serene images of farmland in her native Russia. "See, Lou, is not all bad, still lots wheat, corn, lots food in most countries. Not perfect, sure, but not all bad, *da*? Yes?"

"Dahh, Tanya, but not all good either. If we want to grow lots of food we need genetically modified organisms for inflated crops, lots of pesticide and fertilizer creating lots of toxicity and maybe lots of cancer, and more and more fresh water which is already running short. Did I tell you what's happened to the glaciers in the Himalayas and the Andes?"

Three heads nodded *yes*.

"OK, OK. But then there's oil."

"Olive oil?" said Antonio.

"No, sorry, Antonio," said Lou, handing an empty glass to his old friend. Two ginger ales in one night meant serious business for Lou. "I mean petroleum, fossil fuels, gasoline, coal, natural gas. Agriculture uses huge amounts for farming and transportation. Millions of years to create an irreplaceable resource, the net energy gleaned from the good old sun over an eternity, and all we can think of doing is to dig it all up and set fire to it as fast as possible, leaving nothing for the future of our children and grandchildren. They'll love us for being so frugal. Now, do you want the good news?"

Tanya, Joe and Antonio nodded in unison.

"We're starting to run out. Oil production has peaked, and now it's going down, like it or not. Score one for Mother Earth. Our oil-based economy is about to collapse, but the air might be a little bit cleaner."

"Lou, must say you seem very, very depressed. Worst since you out of, you know, hospital? *Da*?"

"No, I'm not depressed, I'm not down on myself, I am just being realistic, and perhaps slightly saddened at the state of the world.

3

What may look like depression to you and the headshrinkers is what I call an unflinching look at the reality of the horrendous prospects for the future. What do I have to do, provide footnotes? The shrinks gave up trying to treat a nonexistent depression, so they let me out eventually. Probably because they couldn't stand having me around souring the mood of all the other patients and staff. So, I'm still on medical leave, and for now I'm not even supposed to carry around my little 9 millimetre friend." Lou opened his coat to show where his holster used to hang. "They worry that I might sometime get a great notion to pull the trigger and shuffle off my mortal coil, travel to the undiscover'd country and never return. Sorry, I'm mixing metaphors again."

"Lou, is not normal be so obsessed like this," said Tanya.

"At least I don't pretend to be normal, whatever that is."

"Maybe you just need to get back to work, keep busy thinking about something else," said Joe. "Like I always say, it's no good to think too much about things."

"The devil, he make-a work for ideal-a hand," said Antonio.

"Sure, distraction sometimes works, but always temporarily."

Tanya cracked her knuckles, and said, "Lou, I think know what is problem. You take on to own shoulders all problems in world. Many people work at these problems, why *you* must fix everything? National leaders, UN, NGOs, all study and come up with reasonable goals and make policies. Trust they know what they do-ink."

"What's that saying you like, Tanya? *Doh very ein*, something—"

"*Doveryay, no proveryay.* Trust but verify. Is Russian proverb to live by."

"Exactly. Sure, we trust all those good people of immaculate, unimpeachable integrity at the UN and the G20 and all the NGOs and so on. But when we try to verify, things start to appear a little less certain and a lot more murky. Sure, we study, create wonderful sounding things like *Millennium Goals* or *21st Century Plans*, we reach accords in Kyoto and discords in Copenhagen, and how many of those targets are actually achieved? Where is the real progress on climate change?"

"But it's just going to take a little time. Cut 'em some slack, Lou," said Joe.

"We don't have the time! Nature doesn't care how difficult the politics or economics is, it only cares about the laws of physics, chemistry and biology. In a relatively short period of time, we've gone from being small tribes of hunter gatherers to a high tech global society, and we're simply not cognitively equipped to deal with this kind of problem. It would be easier if there was somebody or something we could just shoot, but who do we shoot? Everybody? It all caught up with us too quickly and it's about to collapse like a house of cards. I'm not blaming anyone in particular, and democracy is a wonderful thing, just swell, but democratic governments sometimes seem to be only interested in what will win the next election. Usually that means borrowing more money to give it away, driving nations toward bankruptcy, and showering voters with trinkets."

"Lou, think all new technology, electric cars, energy efficient housing, every day something new. Is progress, no?"

"Tanya, I was hoping you would bring that up. We want someone, some scientist or engineer, to solve our problems. And we only want nice simple solutions, not anything that would make us feel uncomfortable. Listen: who here would like a nice, new electric car, leather upholstery, great acceleration, and non polluting so you can give yourself a merit badge for saving the planet?"

"Sure!"

"*Da.*"

"Do they come in-a green?"

"Right, that's about what I expected. Now who would like to stop driving altogether to save the planet?" Lou paused, allowing a response which did not come. "Neither would I. If no one else is doing anything, why should I bother?" Silence.

Joe had the least tolerance for silence and spoke first. "So now what, Lou? I give up. What do we do?"

"We do what comes naturally to humans, we resort to psychological defences. We pretend it's not happening so we can carry on with business as usual, and leave it all to future generations to solve the big problems, and they will thank us for the mess they inherit. Let's recycle our cans and plant a few trees and pretend that if we all do a little, it will all be just hunky-dory."

Lou took a deep breath before shifting into high gear.

"The problem is so huge and overwhelming we're all in a state of denial, so we keep doing the things we're comfortable doing. We talk and talk, conduct more studies, and talk some more, but nobody, not one single person on earth, has any single, feasible, practical idea to save the living planet before it's too late. I would give anything, absolutely anything, for one good idea."

"Lou, there's got to be some people out there with some good ideas," said Joe. "We put a man on the moon! If we're smart enough to get into this mess, we gotta be smart enough to get out of it, don't we? Somebody will think of something. Won't they?"

Antonio joined Lou and Tanya in a horizontal *No* head shake.

"There is no hope, there is no future, there is no *joie de vivre*. We have nothing, dear friends, nothing to look forward to except madness and death. The world is not merely mad, it is utterly raving, psychotic and deranged beyond salvation, and humanity, *Homo sapiens sapiens* as we like to think of ourselves, the untold billions of stinking bodies motivated purely by self-serving primal drives of preservation and reproduction, can look forward only to horrible, prolonged suffering and death of unimaginable torment from dehydration, starvation, or pandemic disease, putrefying, necrotic flesh wasting away cell by cell, writhing in agony, gasping for breath as we drown in our own precious bodily fluids, until the ultimate blindingly awful white bolt of pain as the heart attacks itself in futile fibrillation and we finally surrender to our inevitable entropic doom and disintegrate to the chaotic elementary particles from which we arose."

Joe had his eyes closed and his hands held tightly over his mouth. Tanya pressed her palms to her ears.

Antonio picked up the TV remote again, and gave Lou a friendly squeeze on the shoulder. "Let's think about some-a thing else, eh?" He flipped through a few channels until he found a news show.

"Hey, that-a guy is plenty good, seem like nice old man," said Antonio. On the ECO TV channel, the grandfatherly, reassuring smile of Neville Lear had an immediate relaxing effect on most people.

"And we eagerly anticipate celebrating the official birth of the eight billionth person to be born on Earth Day, later this month," said Neville in his best BBC-trained voice. "It seems like only yesterday we reached seven billion, but with several corrections of demographic estimates in recent years, here we are, one big happy family of eight billion souls, God bless us, everyone." He shuffled his papers and turned to a different camera angle.

"Other news is of a more lugubrious nature, unfortunately, as yet another mysterious epidemic has occurred, this time in the isolated outer island of Ni'ihau, Hawaii."

The establishing shot showed the tiny Hawaiian island in all its tropical splendour. The screen then dissolved to a wide shot from a helicopter, showing a feeding frenzy of reporters held at bay by police barriers. A few hundred yards off, in a tiny village, workers in white biohazard suits with the CDC logo carried a body bag to an army helicopter. Other medical and military personnel argued with each other in mass confusion.

Neville continued. "Authorities are completely baffled, but assure us that they are doing everything possible to deal with the epidemics. We now join ECO TV journalist Solange du Morgue, live from Ni'ihau, Hawaii."

The expertly coiffed and stylishly dressed Solange appeared out of place in the tropical setting. "It remains a mystery why such deadly epidemics should occur in remote islands with little traffic with the rest of the world. Today's victims are the third confirmed outbreak of an utterly mysterious plague, following episodes in the outer Falkland Islands and in the northern part of Baffin Island. Authorities are meeting in London as we speak. Now back to Neville Lear and the ECO TV News Team."

Neville offered a reassuring smile to everyone in TV land. "It may look grim, with epidemic outbreaks occurring again, but I would like to remind our viewers what my beloved grandmother used to say: *Never fear, never worry, Mother Nature will always find a way to save the day.*"

As the deep tones of Big Ben struck 11 PM, Sir William Muggeridge-Pepys turned his attention from the deafening cacophony to the Palace of Westminster, clearly visible from the discreet, elegantly appointed meeting room. The Minister would be disappointed, extremely disappointed, if he had nothing to report to the Commons regarding this series of epidemics. There was nothing to show for a very long day of negotiations, save frayed nerves and deepening of resentments.

The press sometimes referred to senior diplomats, such as the members of this group, as "Sherpas," but Sir William thought that visually impaired, deaf, lame and developmentally delayed Sherpas would be more accurate. They were mainly career diplomats, but had arrived at these heights of diplomacy not so much for their skill and relevant experience as for their politically correct representation of ages, races and sex, and for a talent for using splendid words to signify nothing of substance. Perhaps that could be advantageous.

He scanned the room to see who had offended whom among his colleagues. Pakistan found India's anti-Muslim overtones offensive, India found China's aggressive water management offensive, China found Japan's re-writing of history offensive, Japan found all of Europe offensive for reasons they were too polite to speak of, and naturally everyone found the Americans offensive for being too American. The American delegate's response was to warn the rest of the world that the G20, like other international organizations, was in danger of becoming irrelevant. Canada was already irrelevant and too boring to be of interest. The Italian delegate said nothing, but continued his endless calculations of something or other.

Sir William stroked his pencil thin white moustache and signalled to the elderly Italian, Sergio Spenalzo, and the rotund Canadian, Jean Brulé, to join him for yet another cup of dreadful tea prepared from colonial teabags.

In the antechamber to the meeting room he poured for his colleagues and offered an opening gambit. "All of this is truly unproductive. With the public pressure mounting we must be seen to be doing something, anything at all."

Spenalzo and Brulé nodded assent.

Sir William continued. "Perhaps what we need to do is to send someone to investigate these epidemics, but not allow his work to be impeded by a lot of media attention, all hugger mugger, *hmm*? But most certainly we must not dispatch a line officer for whom we might be responsible; that could be our undoing. Rather, suppose we sent someone with some sort of, ah, element of deniability, should things become a touch sticky. By outsourcing the investigative services to an independent agent, we cannot be expected to be responsible for the outcome. We can thus be seen to have acted responsibly and with due diligence, and yet we can still be completely irresponsible."

Mutton-chopped Brulé plunked in with the subtlety of a lumberjack. "*D'accord!* It's all in da optics, *eh?* Den we can say we are doing some-ting but can still deny we do any-ting. Sometime doing some-ting is doing no-ting, and vice-versa. Maybe we get lucky and some-ting come from no-ting; or maybe it's the other way 'round. At least we get out of dis stinking room and tell bosses we do some-ting, but cover our *derrières* plenty good, *hein? Parfait!*"

The spindly Sergio Spenalzo set aside his notepad and stared at Brulé.

Sir William interrupted the awkward silence. "Spenalzo, still doing those incomprehensible calculations, are you? What did you call them, a different sort of equation?"

"Differential equations, ordinary, sometimes partial," replied Spenalzo. "An eccentric pastime of mine. Forgive my staring, Brulé, but I was merely lost in thought. Gentlemen, I do believe you are on to something. We need someone independent from the official lines of responsibility. Brulé, you told me once you have an Italian-Canadian fellow you have used a number of times, a gloomy melancholic type, had some sort of breakdown. Lucio, Louis, something like that."

"Luigi Gubriace! Pretty weird guy, but he got lot of contacts all over da place, can keep tings quiet. He's no super spy James Bond, dat for sure. Dat guy used to do some good tings but on disabled list now, and end up in da loony bin. Shrinks kick him out 'cause he make whole mental hospital too depressed. Five minutes in a room wit him and you ready to blow your brain out. Dey call him Lou Gubrious."

"Splendid idea, Brulé," said Sir William. "If he fails, we can say he had another nervous breakdown, poor chap. He might even have an unfortunate fatal accident, if absolutely necessary. Should he succeed, then we have not only solved the mystery of the plagues but further advanced the noble cause of hiring the mentally handicapped. I'll call the meeting to order and bring it to a close."

Sir William zipped up his slim attaché case, and added as an afterthought, "We might send someone to tag along with him, provide him some support if he is a tad wonky. I know of a Dr. Jillian Fleming, forensic psychiatrist, and her superlative interrogation skills might prove handy. She broke the *Al-Jebrah* ringleader with no obvious rough stuff. The very person to keep a sharp eye on Mr. Gubbey-whatever, and assist in the investigation."

"H'okay!" said Brulé as he began to place a call on his cell phone.

Sergio Spenalzo merely smiled, nodded and began work on another differential equation.

Back at Antonio's, Lou was almost finished.

". . . and if that, the unspeakable reality, is impossible, and it truly is, then there is absolutely no hope and we are doomed. That's how the world as we know it must end. End of story."

"Lou, must be some other way. Is always hope, *da*?"

"You don't *like* how our world is going to end? Then show me another way—and please, no *deus ex machina* fairy tale ending," said Lou. "Oops—hold that thought, Tanya."

Lou pulled his vibrating cell phone from his pocket.

The display showed the single word: *Brulé*.

"Sorry, the story is not over yet."

CHAPTER 2

To the Bahamas and Cuba

"Luigi Gubriace!?" said Jill as she stepped from a non-polluting electric taxi. She stared at the gargantuan figure of Omar "Joe" Falooka as he heaved the last of the cargo onto the small private jet at Burpelson airfield. The 6 foot, 8 inch, 350 pound Egyptian giant pointed to the cabin's interior and leapt up the steps ahead of her.

"Up here," said Lou, poking his head out of the plane. "Dr. Jillian Fleming? Jill?"

Jill nodded, grabbed her bags and rushed up the steps to board the plane.

"Hurry up, we don't have a second to waste," said Lou.

As Joe took the pilot's seat, she quickly surveyed the small plane and took the seat opposite Lou.

"Luigi Gubriace. Call me Lou, please.

"Jill, we almost have left without you," said Tanya, emerging from behind the pile of cargo in the rear of the jet. Tanya took the seat between Lou and the cockpit and pulled a white laptop computer from her bag, never losing sight of Jill.

"Joe, let's get crackink," said Tanya, smiling.

"Joe Falooka," Lou explained to the astonished Jill. "Former Egyptian heavyweight boxing champion." He leaned in to whisper into Jill's ear. "Really nice guy, but you must, absolutely, must never, ever, use foul language near Joe."

"I am Tanya. Tanya Chekhov. Working with Lou and Joe many times. We are having lucky break; now Lou will explain." Tanya opened her computer and began to type fiercely as the jet took off.

"Lou, I'm awfully sorry, but I'm still quite in the dark about all this. I know it's all about these wretched epidemics, but Sir William Muggeridge-Pepys said—"

"Mr. Mucky-Pup. I should have guessed," said Lou.

"Sir William said you would explain, so perhaps we could take a few minutes to fill me in, *hmm*?"

"All in good time. First, I'm going to put you to work. I hear you're good at reading people, and we need an unbiased, professional opinion on this recording. The sound quality is just awful, but it's all we've got. Tanya?"

Tanya handed Jill a cell phone and helped her with the headset attachment. "Poor audio quality is better on headphones, easier to hear over noise of plane taking off, but still very stinky sound. Just say what you hear, then give opinion."

Jill took a few seconds to adjust the headset and compose herself. Lou and Tanya were watching her closely. She pushed the *Play* button and closed her eyes.

"All right, here goes. '*Lou—* . . . *get to Kubrick I . . . Bah . . . epidemics . . . evi—. . . not . . . sick, getting . . . out, batteries . . . dead . . . Lou . . . patho—. . . PS . . . near . . .* ' The quality is awful and it's mostly static. Who's Kubrick?"

"Not who, where. Kubrick Island, Bahamas. That part is easy. What else?" said Lou.

Jill replayed the message, listening before speaking. "Problems with the batteries, obviously, which partially accounts for the detestable quality. Something to do with the epidemics, related to the pathology."

"Or the pathogens responsible for the disease," said Lou.

13

"Someone is feeling sick, sounds like the speaker, maybe others, and someone or something dead, maybe the batteries, maybe someone on the island. American accent, southern, probably from North Carolina, plus an overlay of a Harvard education. He said *evidently* or *evidence*, ruddy difficult to guess which, and he says Lou twice. He knows you well but not intimately, not family. A close friend?"

"I recognized the voice. The call was from a colleague, Herb Thicket, one of my best contacts, and he went to MIT, not Harvard. Otherwise, very well done, Jill. How was his emotional state?"

"Not much to go on, without knowing him or hearing more. Fairly high level of anxiety, high strung, maybe a nervous laugh lost in the static, but excited about something positive, some good news."

"That sounds like Herb; he's full of energy when he gets an idea."

Jill listened again. "The post script said something about *near*, near to what, a location or near to knowing something?"

"It's not like Herb to say P.S. in an oral message, he's more casual. Anything else?"

"No. I'll listen again on the way, but I very much doubt I shall be able to fill in all the blanks," said Jill, putting down the headset. "Lou, if we're dealing with another outbreak, shouldn't we wait for the local authorities, police, public health, to go into the site first?"

"That's what's happened at every other location, and it's been bungled. After three outbreaks they can't even identify the pathogen. Doesn't that make you suspicious? Why are the best experts coming up empty? *Hmmm?* My primary contact said they wanted a completely independent investigation, with no room for interference or sabotage, and for that we'll do it ourselves and with contacts I can trust. And, now, thanks to Herb, we can literally fly in under the radar before the press gets wind of it. Public attention is the last thing we need."

Jill watched Lou rub his hands nervously, and open and close his seatbelt several times, eyes darting.

Joe turned on the autopilot and did a sleight-of-hand trick for Tanya, pulling a coin from her ear and turning it into a small flower. He glanced at Lou and said, "Hey, Lou, wanna take the helm for a while? Get your mind off things?"

"Why not? Better to die in a plane crash than from the plague." He turned on the cockpit stereo, and the strains of *Figaro* filled the plane.

"Here we all are, Jill," muttered Lou as he took the co-pilot's seat, "cast adrift on a ship of fools, flying off to oblivion, wallowing in the mire of a sterile, godless, utterly absurd universe only to suffer and die in agony and isolation. We are in fact just a bunch of half-wit primates, too clever for our own good yet not clever enough, in reality nothing but a fortuitous concourse of atoms . . ."

Kubrick Island was rumoured to have been once owned by a pop music icon of the 1960s, a safe place to hide from the public and the media, a tropical paradise for romance and a no man's land for very private meetings. Now, it was a private resort for a highly select clientele, available only by referral. This night, four figures in white biohazard suits with filtration ventilators walked silently from the airstrip to the main lodge. Despite the setting sun, no birds sang.

Lou gestured for Joe to enter first, automatic pistol in hand. Then Lou slowly stepped in, and stood in silent observation for almost a minute, before allowing Jill and Tanya to bring in the technical gear. A deathly silence enveloped the luxurious drawing room. Lou tried the lights, but the power was out. With a flashlight, he saw several bodies lying on couches and on the floor, apparently seeking some sort of comfort or camaraderie in their last hours. A uniformed butler lay beside a rosewood cart bearing water, juices, glasses, bottles of

Aspirin and Tylenol. The waste containers overflowed with still moist tissues, an FPS shipping carton serving as an additional container for the deadly waste. The victims' clothing was stained with saliva, blood, and fluid spewed from their respiratory systems.

"I count six bodies here," said Lou, his voice distorted by the ventilator of his biohazard suit, gesturing the number six. "Saliva and blood samples please, labels and photographs, identification if we can find it. Otherwise we must not disturb the scene."

"They appear to have been dead only one or two hours," said Jill, examining the first two corpses. "Colour changes, temperature not too far down in this heat, some rigor mortis, no bloating yet. Apart from the fluid stains, the clothing is fairly fresh, suggesting it came on rather quickly."

As Joe stood guard near the door, the other three figures moved about on soft-soled shoes, examining the bodies, carefully taking samples. The only sound was the muffled breathing through the ventilators. Lou briefly contemplated the grim reality that all that stood between him and near certain death was a thin, 89 cent plastic filter in his ventilator, supplied by the lowest bidder.

Lou turned one body over for a closer look.

"Here he is," he said. "This is—*was*—Herb Thicket, the one who made the call. I don't think I know the others." He looked at Jill and added, "Let's finish and get out of here before the *authorities* show up."

Jill and Tanya opened two containers labelled *Liquid Nitrogen* and a heavy white mist spilled out, quickly covering much of the floor.

Lou moved silently from room to room on both floors with his flashlight, checking closets, under beds, shower stalls, anywhere a live victim might have been hiding, anywhere a further clue might be found. He eventually returned to the drawing room, and said, "Nothing elsewhere, no one else. They all came together at the end."

"Lou, behind staircase may be closet or cellar stairs, this too please check," said Tanya.

He found a door marked *Staff Only*, twisted the doorknob, and heard a low, growling noise.

"Hey! Someone may still be—"

Lou had only partially opened the door when a large, drooling, snarling Rottweiler leapt several feet, his fangs aimed directly for the throat. Lou blocked the attack with his shoulder as they tumbled in a circular arc.

Tanya gasped in horror. "Lou, no! Joe! Joe!"

Joe had already taken aim, and with a quiet *pfffft!* from his silenced pistol the dog gave out a final yelp, and a spurt of blood sprayed Lou's suit.

Jill raced over and examined Lou's shoulder. "His suit has been torn open. We've got to disinfect everyone and go—NOW!"

Lou clutched his shoulder and shouted, "Tanya, take everything we've got. It's the only real evidence we have."

Joe scooped up Lou with one arm and the odd quartet raced back to the airstrip.

Soon the jet soared through the night sky while the stereo played the *Papagena* duet. Joe kept an eye on the autopilot as he and Tanya played "rock, paper, scissors" in the cockpit.

Jill finished her examination and said to Lou, "Fortunately the skin wasn't broken, and I think we're all safely disinfected. If we were playing by the book we should all get into quarantine."

"Joe, how long until we get to Montez?"

"We should be there in 27 minutes, Lou."

"Montez?"

Lou turned back to Jill. "Montez and I go back for years and he's the best in Cuba. He's treated Fidel, Raoul, and lots of celebrities.

He owes me a few favours, and best of all, he never asks too many questions."

"Lou, can *you* answer a few more questions?" asked Jill. "Who exactly are you working with—"

"Sorry, but you'll get all you need to know as we go. Losing Herb was a major setback, so right now our priority has to be getting the samples analyzed, ASAP. Montez can help expedite it after he checks us ov—"

Lou started coughing, spat up a bit of phlegm, and quickly put on a medical mask.

Jill observed him closely and said, "You're sweating, and your breathing is strained. Lou . . . what's happening?"

"It's nothing really, probably just some food poisoning. Sorry. Hot . . . nausea . . . headache . . ."

"It doesn't look like food poisoning to me and even if you picked up something there your immune system can't possibly react this quickly. It's been less than an hour since we left the lodge. Masks back on everyone! Joe?!"

"Going as fast as we can. Hang on, Lou."

Lou slumped backward and rolled one eyelid open, punctuating the events of the day with a Cyclops stare at Jill.

The double doors of the Zapata Clinic crashed open as two paramedics rushed Lou's gurney to an isolation unit. Jill, Joe and Tanya followed closely behind, still wearing their masks. A small team of nurses began attending to Lou, setting up an intravenous line and taking vital signs.

Dr. Garcia Montez was a short, middle-aged Hispanic whose thick eyebrows, moustache and black horn-rimmed glasses gave him a passing resemblance to Groucho Marx. Garcia pushed his way into the melee and shook Lou by his good shoulder, reviving him.

"Lou? *Amigo?* You can hear me?"

"Garcia, thank God," Lou whispered, coughing. "It hurts when I cough."

"Come on Lou, I am not impressed by your cough. You have one very nice wheeze, though."

Jill spoke up from the doorway. "This is impossible. He was infected less than two hours ago."

"Speedy work, Lou," said Montez. "Vital signs?"

"Temp 39.9 Celsius, pulse racing, BP 84 over 48 and dropping," came a voice from the throng of nurses.

"What's happening?" said Lou, his eyes darting.

"I am now guessing, but I think you are having the very bad bacterial infection, and you are heading for the cardiac arrest, and now you are sorry you asked, *si*?" said Montez. "People, please, if you do not need to be here, step to the outside, please, and let the nurses give you the once over. Sanchez, take the people's vitals and run the same tests as for Lou. Stand back and let the big Doc get to work!"

Montez and team continued working, as Joe, Tanya and Jill exchanged "now what?" glances, and retreated to the lounge with Nurse Sanchez.

As the morning sun streamed into the clinic's lounge, Tanya was asleep on a couch, her ever-present computer as a pillow, and Jill was asleep on a parallel couch. Joe sat upright in the largest chair, snoring lightly. Dr. Montez was working at the desk in his office, the door ajar.

Lou walked into the lounge wearing nothing but a hospital gown, brushing his teeth. He gave Joe's chair a push and said "Wakey-wakey. Rise and shine!"

Joe awoke with a loud snort and shouted, "LOU?!?"

Tanya rubbed her eyes in disbelief. "Lou! We thought you dying! How you feel? You okay?"

"Small headache, large appetite," said Lou. "Garcia—Dr. Montez, what the, what just happened?"

"I do not know! This is almost 30 years I am treating infectious diseases, never have I seen anything like this. Your infection just disappeared, *poof!* and your immune system has rebooted itself to normal."

"Disappeared?" said Jill. "That's impossible!"

"Lou, if we were doing this officially I would legally be obliged to put all four of you into quarantine, but your vitals are all fine. Whatever you have had is acting fast, so I do not think anyone else has been infected with this very strange bug. *Amigo*, you want you should stay here for observation?" said Montez.

"Thanks Doc, but we have to get going. Sorry." Lou returned to his room and began retrieving his clothes. He flipped the TV channels until he found the ECO TV international news channel in English.

Jill pulled Dr. Montez back into his office for a short conference.

"Dr. Montez, are you certain it's bacterial? Have you identified the species?"

"We do not have the facilities here, but I will get all your samples on the priority Canadian flight to the National Microbiology Laboratory in Winnipeg, later today. It's one of the best Level 4 infectious disease labs in the world. Sorry, I must to get back to work. *Via con dios.*"

"Thanks, awfully. You've been a brick," said Jill, scurrying to Lou's room.

"*De nada.*" Montez returned to the admitting area to attend to another patient in a wheelchair.

Joe whispered to Tanya "Check that new guy out. He looks like he could be Lou's brother."

Jill knocked on Lou's door.

"Come in," said Lou, buttoning his shirt, his eyes still glued to the TV. "Have a look at this guy, Mendel. I don't know why he's so popular. He's always being interviewed on TV these days."

Jill gave the screen a cursory glance and said, "Oh, that guy. He's just another trendy celebrity, enjoying his 15 minutes of fame. Next week it will be someone selling everyone on an eco-friendly vegan diet to save the world. But how about you? Are you fit for travel?"

"Super. I'll catch some sleep on the plane and we'll brainstorm at my office. Have you any idea how I could fall so ill so quickly, and recover completely, all in a matter of hours?"

Jill shrugged and said, "I haven't the foggiest idea. There is so much we don't know about our own bodies. Perhaps you have an extraordinarily robust immune system, perhaps you were exposed to a similar bug years ago and acquired some immunity, or maybe you're just uncommonly lucky. Optimism is always good for you. I recommend keeping a positive outlook. Always look on the bright side of life, Lou."

"I've looked. There is no bright side."

"Perhaps the lab results will help us turn up something," said Jill with her best bedside manner smile.

"Maybe, but in the meanwhile we need to generate some fresh ideas."

Lou and Jill joined Tanya and Joe and they left the clinic. The TV in Lou's room was left on, as the interview continued.

In the ECO TV studio, the monitors faded in the caption *Sapphira Jones Live with Guest Dr. Karl Mendel*, and dissolved to a tight two-shot. Sapphira had chosen a new couch for her world-famous guest, a love seat with an earthy green tone to highlight her new earthy green suit and natural silk, chartreuse hosiery. She could not stand the sexual tension any longer, and snuggled up to Karl's tall, athletic frame, her bushy Afro teasing his left earlobe. A soft *Oooohhh!* whooshed through the mainly earth-toned, mainly female, and totally politically correct studio audience. Karl merely flashed his gleaming, perfect teeth in her direction, stroked her hand, and continued addressing the camera directly with his devilishly hypnotic pale blue eyes.

"You are so absolutely right, Sapphira, I just *love* the way you think, and I *love* being on your show with this marvellous audience. As we all saw in the clip from the video, *The Brutal, Vicious and Heartless Corporate Rape of Our Mother Earth*, uninhibited, unregulated, unimpeded, and unfeeling logging and burning are devastating the rainforests in both the equatorial and temperate regions at an alarming rate. We are not only destroying an irreplaceable resource, but the logging industry continually builds roads into the primordial jungle. This has created a biological super highway for countless micro-organisms to reach the entire planet. Now we have unleashed bacteria, viruses, and fungi, the sources of horrible, painful and often fatal diseases, previously unknown to most of humanity. Furthermore, with jet travel, pathogens can catch a ride on a human and zoom to anywhere on the planet within a day. You and I, and our viewers at home, have had no previous exposure to these tropical diseases and hence no natural immunity. We are completely at their mercy."

"So, Dr. Mendel," said Sapphira, straightening up, "these very peculiar diseases that we've seen recently are simply further evidence of the ruthless corporate man's brutal exploitation of the planet."

"Exactly, Sapphira, but don't lose heart! We can all do something to help. It's too easy to give in to a feeling of powerlessness. I may be only one little person out of eight billion, but if we all pull together, we can do it! *Can-do! Can-do!* At the Mendel Foundation, we know how to find the answer. The answer is inspired by *love*, *love* for each other, yourself, and the whole living planet, and the *love* is disseminated by education. Education, for boys, girls, adults, seniors, for every single, living breathing human on earth, even the corporate executives who are the object of so much animosity. *Love* comes first, and the education will then flow forth freely and naturally. Love is the only real, true teacher, and only love can heal the mind, heal the planet. No one in his right mind ever consciously sets out to rapaciously destroy the environment, our loving Mother Earth."

"Please, Dr. Mendel, tell me—tell us all—what to do! We all want to help you, don't we, people?"

The studio audience exploded in applause, cheers, and cries of "Yes! Tell us! Show us the way, please!" A weak voice in the back uttered, "Take me, Karl, take me now!" before subsiding to a low moan.

"There is so much *love* in this room, Sapphira, it's an inspiration; I feel so unworthy to be in the presence of such a beautiful, wonderful audience, and in all humility, I am so honoured to be the guest of a truly superlative, gracious hostess and goddess of beauty, Sapphira." The audience sighed in unison, and Sapphira snuggled closer again, her hand gripping his thigh, her rate of respiration increasing.

"But the message is so simple and yet so profound. We need to change our relationship with Mother Earth, and become responsible, caring stewards of the living planet. It's mainly a matter of adopting the conserving lifestyle. We can recycle, use energy efficient light bulbs, we can ride a bicycle to work, or we can plant trees. We can not, we must not, and we shall not be pessimists."

"Oh, Dr. Mendel, Karl," Sapphira cooed, "I could listen to you all day, but I'm getting a signal from our producer. Our viewers can find lots of great ideas on the Mendel Foundation website, can't they, Karl?"

Karl took Sapphira's hand, held it close to his chest, and turned to face the TV camera directly, and brushed a tear from his eye.

"Sapphira, everyone at home," he said, gently biting his lower lip and taking a slow, dramatic breath, "It's up to all of us, every single one of the eight billion of us, to do everything, anything we possibly can, if we truly love this planet.

CHAPTER 3

Not in Canada, Lou

Had a blind man wandered into the ECO TV newsroom by mistake he would have been forgiven for thinking he was in a miniature stock exchange, or perhaps a special little circle of hell reserved for the acoustically sensitive. Reporters, writers, videographers, technicians and the flotsam and jetsam of the TV world were holding impromptu meetings, yakking on telephones, and pounding vigorously on keyboards, all the while keeping an eye on their own network monitors and transmissions from their competitors. The only acceptable response to the constant din was to shout louder and slurp more coffee with more noisy vigour. Only a few of the media aristocracy, such as Neville Lear, rated quiet, private, wood-panelled offices on the upper floors.

Woody Logan sometimes regretted having made the quantum leap from the relatively civilized world of college radio and newspapers to the electronic jungle of the ECO TV multimedia enterprise. With a finger in his right ear and his desk phone to his left, he tried to hear what a confidential source was telling him.

"This is fantastic, unbelievable," he shouted, "and they got this information how? . . . You've got to be kidding . . . No way . . . and they got the number from that? Who was the plane registered to?"

Woody stole a glance at the adjacent desk, where his videographer, Clarisse "Punky" Von Neuman, rolled yet another joint, number six or seven so far today. Woody didn't care if she was the daughter of corporate vice-president Vladimir Von Neuman, this kid was not going to drive today.

"He's what—you're kidding!" said Woody, scribbling down a few notes with a pencil. "Give me his description and the address so I can surprise this guy, get a candid firsthand account . . . 40 plus or minus, average build, looks like a sadsack Italian waiter . . . yeah, I know the intersection, second floor. . . . Yeah, . . . hey, if I can land this one I might get a little r-e-s-p-e-c-t around here. I owe you big time, buddy."

Punky stowed her reefers into her camera bag and began buffing her black fingernails, nose ring and dog collar spikes with a lens cleaning cloth.

"Fantastic, I gotta get on this *tout de suite*," said Woody. He covered the mouthpiece of his phone and whispered "Punky!" as he stood up and counted down from five with his fingers.

"Later, man," said Woody, hanging up as he stood to put on his preppy blazer.

"Who was that, Woodsy?" said Punky, scooping up her bag and camera.

"A super confidential source from my carefully guarded network of informants. Let's go, this is an unbelievably hot one." He took another look at Punky's dilated pupils and added, "I'm driving this time."

"Yo, Woodster!" shouted Sapphira Jones, sneaking up behind him and grabbing his buttocks with both hands. "You got a hot one? A hot what?"

"Dang-it Sapphira," said Woody, "Paws off, please. This story won't keep."

Sapphira started rubbing his shoulders. "I did my one-on-one with Karl Mendel this morning, and I am still so high from the vibes even little *Woodenheimer* is lookin' mighty fine." She stole a tiny nibble from his well scrubbed ear lobe.

"My name is Woodrow, or Woody, Sapphira, and please stop yanking my—just lay off the sexual harassment stuff."

Sapphira ran her fingers through Woody's brush cut, pinched his cheeks and made a kissy face a few millimetres from his lips. "Getting it on, Wood-pecker? Oh, Woody-Woodstein-Wood-dink-o-vitch!"

Woody turned a dark shade of scarlet, and said in his broadcast voice, "Really, gotta run. I got the inside scoop on the latest plague outbreak and I've got to nail this guy before the competition gets wind of it." He picked up his briefcase and pulled free from Sapphira's grasp. "Punky and I are going with it live on the next newscast."

"Another plague!? Go for it *Woodsman*, go man go! But don't forget to clear it with Neville," shouted Sapphira. "Nothing goes on the air without his OK, especially live."

"Don't worry; I just know he's going to love this. I'm already approved for a live broadcast, so I'm just going to switch stories. And hold on to those good vibrations for later," he said with a wink, squeezing out the door with Punky.

"I hope you know what you're doing, Wood-chopper," said Punky. "I just point and shoot."

The mid-morning traffic was light on the expressway as a black stretch limousine weaved its way toward the airport. The consistently dour-faced DeWang, a uniformed chauffeur and gentleman's gentleman, kept his eyes on the road and his attention off his employer in the passenger compartment. The only personal touch he allowed was a small dashboard photo of his late parents, Booker and Xiao-Yan.

Behind the soundproof, frosted privacy window, Karl Mendel was in an animated conversation on his high security, encrypted phone.

"The usual, you know, go ride a bike, plant a few trees and everything will be hunky-dory. They always buy some easy nonsense if I don't ask them to do anything the slightest bit difficult. I don't dare suggest that we need to make any big changes that threaten anyone's lifestyle or I'll lose my grassroots support base. I did take a fancy to that woman from the local station, though. Sapphira something or other. I must make sure we take care of her somehow."

From a private line on the other side of the pond, Sir William Muggeridge-Pepys' polite voice responded to Karl's digressions. "Absolutely, always room for one more, what? Fine looking woman, to be sure. But about the Sherpas, Karl, I must bring you up to date."

"Yes, Sir William, how have they decided to proceed? Anything to worry about?"

"I have some good news, I dare say. For a while I was concerned they might pick an investigative team who knew a little something about epidemiology, microbiology, that sort of technical twaddle. I was able to convince a couple of malleable sorts to choose an independent agent, someone completely incompetent and expendable."

"Excellent work, Sir William, we can always count on a committee to arrive at the worst possible decision. The IQ of a group is inversely proportional to the number of members, isn't that what they say? So, who's leading the investigation?"

"If I may be so bold, I do believe you will approve. The Canadians have some poor, mentally ill chap that no one would miss. My best guess is that he is likely to muddle about ineffectually for weeks or months and have nothing to show for it. Italian sounding name, Louie, Linguine, Gobreezie, Gooberasey, something like that. Ah, yes, Gubriace, rhymes with Liberace."

"You don't mean to say . . . Luigi Gubriace?" said Karl, as he felt the blood drain from his face.

"Yes, that's it. I had a premonition you would be pleased."

"Lou Gubrious? You never heard about him? He gives the impression of being an incompetent ass, but he somehow always manages to pull it off. Sir William, have you any idea what sort of connections this man has?"

"Not precisely, no, but the Canadian, Brulé did say something about odd contacts or whatever. No one ever understands what Brulé is talking about. Seems to have a congenital language disorder. Very useful trait in diplomacy, I must say."

"Forget about Brulé and focus on Lou Gubrious. He somehow always finds someone who is in the know. Do you appreciate how dangerous this is? What if Lou Gubrious picks up the trail? Where is he now?"

"Not precisely sure where they are at present. They went to Cuba and may still be there, or perhaps by now they are in your part of the world. Ah, yes, some more good news. I took the liberty of inserting a mole into his team. Keeping us informed on the sly, something of a fifth columnist. Could easily throw a spanner into the works, eh what?"

"That may not be enough, and I can't take any chances. I'm sending in the Hip Hop boys," said Karl, reaching for a bottle of iceberg water from the limo's bar.

"Can't say I'm acquainted with them. Hip Hop? Musical chaps?"

"Hip Hop? Musical? I underestimated your talent for oxymorons, Sir William. They're more talented with their machine guns than with their execrable vocal chords. The Hip Hop boys work in small units all over the globe, blending in with the local culture. They tend to be too verbal and absurdly intellectual but they can easily deal with Lou Gubrious."

"Splendid, Karl, splendid, absolutely first rate idea, bit of brain power as well as brawn, so to speak."

Karl pressed a button on the limo's intercom. "Airport, DeWang, and step on it. We've got big problems."

"Very good, sir, we shall accelerate immediately," crackled DeWang's voice over the intercom.

"Now, Sir William," said Karl, "have you any other good news?"

As Lou turned the key to his office door, Jill paused to read the company nameplate: *Gubriace, Leung, Usualuk and MacPherson—Export Consulting.*

"It's just a front," said Lou as he opened the door and entered first, followed by Tanya, then Jill. Lou punched three numbers into a keypad to disarm the security system.

"Oh! 2, 5, 9." said Jill. "My birthday. Sorry, I was being nosy, wasn't I?"

"That's OK; you're just being a good observer. Make yourself at home."

Jill scanned the tiny office, and first noticed a ubiquitous layer of dust, which gave a ghostly aura to the small conference table, a few folding chairs, two computers, and a large screen TV. Several mounted fish and nets adorned the walls, and a golf bag with fishing rods was wedged between two wooden filing cabinets.

"It's sort of a hobby of mine. Fishing, not the taxidermy," said Lou as he removed a stuffed barracuda from a chair, dusted the seat off with his hand, and gestured for Jill to sit.

"Whatever happened to Leung, Usualuk and MacPherson?" said Jill with a wry smile.

"I had them stuffed," said Lou, straight-faced. "Sorry, that was in bad taste, wasn't it?"

"Is no one here just Lou, sometime Joe and me," said Tanya as she plugged in her laptop. She cracked her knuckles twice, cracked her neck once, and cracked her spine against the wooden chair back. "All right, let's get crackink." Tanya began typing furiously.

"Perhaps we could focus on the issue at hand, as time is of the essence. Where shall we commence, Lou?" said Jill.

"Bear with me for a moment, please, but I want to start with me. I came very close to dying, just hours ago, and that has changed—is changing—everything for me. The prospect of dying, or others dying, now has a reality I was unaware of previously. Focus, yes, nothing like a brush with death to focus the mind," said Lou.

"Yes, it was a stressful experience, indubitably, but may I suggest we examine the facts of the situation. What do you think was the true course of events on Kubrick Island?"

"It was most likely the same infection as the previous cases. The victims were all in isolated locations with a very small population, they had some interaction with the rest of the world, but not frequent, and it was all over very quickly. The big difference is that this time I got it too."

"But we're still completely in the dark about the nature of the infections. How can we be so sure that it was the same pathogen?" said Jill. "Perhaps we should just wait for the results from the Winnipeg lab."

"That could take quite a while. The crazy thing is, I got the same bug, and the infection stopped dead in its tracks. Yet all the residents on Kubrick died within a day or even hours of each other. Herb Thicket's last phone call gives us a time frame to work with."

"Your experience was certainly anomalous. In all probability, the infectious agent mutated to a less lethal species by the time we got there. That often happens with micro-organisms," said Jill.

"I thought about that, but Dr. Montez said I was seriously infected, and it was likely a bacterial infection. And even if there were some mutation, it would have to have occurred extraordinarily fast, and in the small, homogeneous environment of the lodge, I would likely have gotten the original bug, the one that killed the others, at the same time. So, a milder mutation would not have saved me."

Lou took a pad of graph paper from a shelf, plunked it in front of Jill, and did a quick pencil sketch of the layout of the lodge. "The airstrip is to the west, we came in through the main doors here, and it was dark inside."

Lou doodled on the pad, adding a door, a few rectangular blobs in the centre for furniture, and an arrow from the door to a doodle representing the light switch. "So, I tried the light switch, nothing happened, and I assumed the power had run out. Maybe it was an old generator and everyone was too sick to fix it. *Hmmm*. The cell phone batteries were running out of juice by the time Herb made his call. *Hmmm*. The bugs were running out of juice by the time they got to me, too. *Hmmm*."

Lou stared at Jill. She stared back, and raised her eyebrows. Lou raised his eyebrows. With no more supercilia to elevate, she said, "So? What's that got to do with anything?"

Lou did a rough sketch of a lumpy bacterium beside the lodge sketch, adding a few blobs in the bug's centre. Then he added a switch. *Hmmm!*

"Think outside the proverbial box for a second. Maybe this bug came equipped with an off switch, or the batteries were running out, and I got the bug just before it stopped ticking."

Jill rolled her eyes and lobbed a sneering guffaw directly at him. "Sorry Lou, but that's utterly preposterous. Bacterial cells are like little machines that suck up nutrients and energy until they get fat enough to split into two little cells. They simply continue to multiply as long as the environment permits, and have done so for billions of years. There is no way they can be made to stop, and they will not stop, provided the supply of food, water, temperature and so on is suitable."

"You're undoubtedly right, but suppose, just suppose for a minute, they were tinkered with in some way so they could be made to stop. Why would someone bother? What's the point?" Lou tried to make eye contact with Jill, but now she was intensely examining the stuffed barracuda.

Tanya whacked a button of her keyboard with a resounding *plunk*. "*Nyet*, Lou, nothing. CIA, MI5, MI6, CSIS, all have investigation, all have meeting, no one has leads. We talk our self to death. Fiddle while Rome is burning."

"I just can't believe no one has identified any of the pathogens by now," said Jill. "The Centres for Disease Control must have tested the samples from Ni'ihau, Hawaii."

"Is very strange. For example, CDC have very good protocols and excellent history but samples from Ni'ihau all corrupt by time they get in CDC lab Atlanta. Best guesses based on gross autopsy of victims; suggest some sort pneumonic plague, maybe very bad strain of *Yersinia pestis*. Is highly infectious airborne bacteria, very high mortality rate, very fast. Maybe when Lou's frozen spits get to Winnipeg is best chance now to identify." Tanya began typing again with renewed vigour.

Lou scratched his chin stubble. "Another anomaly. One of the best labs in the world can't identify a bacterial species."

Tanya stopped typing and said, "Holy smokes, Lou. Now appears similar outbreak in Stromboli, island in Italy, but is much worse. Precisely 40 dead, then plague stop, everyone else who was ill recover in few hours, then seem be OK and just walk away. Like Lou. *Oy vey!*"

Lou looked at Tanya, then at Jill, as all three sat with their mouths slightly open in stunned silence.

Jill jumped when the door burst open with a crash. "Food's here!" shouted Joe. "Time for a late lunch."

Lou fiddled with the TV as Joe started unpacking the food onto the already crowded table. "I got some sandwiches, a few pizzas, sodas, juice, two urns of coffee, a few chickens, couple of pies, falafel, humus, bagels, some subs, Chinese takeout, and some black and green stuff. Take a look Jill; I think it's your Marmite."

Tanya turned to Jill and said, "When food arrive, men stop thinking with brain, think with stomach. Watch, Joe will eat most of food and Lou will munch one sandwich with coffee, turn on TV and become like zombie. He is like catatonic with TV. At least is not depressed when working."

Jill folded her hands on the table and slipped into professorial mode. "That's the best thing for him. He needs to work, or engage in some other intensively preoccupying distraction to help him from slipping into his Hamlet persona. I don't think he's clinically depressed at present, and from what I've seen so far he's hardly impulsive enough to be considered a suicide risk."

"Lou not impulsive, sure, but sometimes mood can change very quick. Sometimes not know what to expect. Except Lou is never jolly with big fat *ho ho ho* like Father Christmas. Lou is not proverbial *Good Humour* man."

"That fits. He does seem to have a classical depressive personality disorder, but I have to be a smidgen cautious, as it has a significant rate of co-morbidity with major depression. He inflicts his negativity on everyone around him. It probably makes him feel better, temporarily, at everyone else's expense."

Tanya gave Jill a double thumbs up and a wink and went back to typing.

Joe had barely finished gobbling up his first chicken when Tanya shouted, "*Eureka!* Lou—I've got somethink! Something about Herb's phone message did not sound right, so I run audio file through most favourite Russian linguistic program to analyze voice patterns. When Herb said "PS" what everyone think?"

"*Post Script*, an afterthought, an extra part of the message added on," said Lou.

"*Da*. Me too. But program say intonation used in 'PS' suggests it was part of longer phrase. Lou, I saw *F*-P-S shipping package at Kubrick resort, just used to hold old snotty tissues from dead peoples, so not think about it at time. Now maybe I think Herb was talking about FPS shipping company. So now have hacked on to FPS database, and find each site of outbreak each receive FPS package labelled 'Electronics' soon before disease start!"

Lou's eyes widened. "Great work, Tanya! Can you find the place of origin? The routes? The shippers?"

"*Da!* Yes yes yes—the shipping routes seem unnecessary complicated, but all were shipped through same FPS office, like focal point, only few miles from here. Clerk's signatures seem be same, but cannot decipher name." Tanya rubbed her hands gleefully and cracked her knuckles again.

Lou set aside the TV remote and slurped the last of his coffee. "We need to find that clerk and ask him a few questions."

"Let me handle the interrogation," said Jill. "I need to pick up a few things, then I shall make him talk."

"Good—I know we can count on you, Jill. Tanya and I will go there first in my Volkswagen, and start with a little pleasant conversation. Joe, take Jill in the Hummer, get what she needs, and make sure we can use the 'Royal Suite.' Don't stop for lunch."

"Gotcha Lou," said Joe, scooping up a few kilograms of food and tossing a sandwich to Tanya. He offered a thick cheese pizza with double garlic, onions, snails, marmite and anchovies to Jill, which she declined with a polite gesture.

In seconds all four were gone, the TV still running. On the screen a caption popped up: *Repeat broadcast—Cookie Lemon with Dr. Karl Mendel.* Cookie tossed her long blond mane and thrust her buxom figure toward Karl, her nipples almost bursting through her too small sweater.

"Absolutely fabulous, luv, quite brilliant. We'd love to hear more, Dr. Mendel, but it's time for our special little guest," she said, and gestured to a zoo attendant. "Look at this, children. This is a Bo-no-bo, and he looks like a little chimpanzee, doesn't he? But he has some very different patterns of behaviour."

"*Aaawww!* Aren't you just the cutest little guy!" said Karl, picking him up and putting him onto his lap. "You know, Cookie, boys and girls, we can all help save cute little guys like Mr. Bonobo here with simple things like not using too much electricity."

Lou rushed back into his office, turned off the lights and TV, and rushed off.

Woody did an illegal U-turn and snatched the only available parking spot near his destination, squeezing the ECO TV hybrid car between a two seater Smart Car and a decrepit blue van with handmade curtains on its windows. The sidewalk in front of the 1960s office low-rise was thick with pedestrians, office workers enjoying the sunshine and the local beggars feigning homelessness. A mixed group of teenagers charged back and forth on skateboards, heedless of the pedestrians. Noises of drinking and laughter came from the curtained van.

"That's the address. Good grief, what a dump. It must be a cover, or a false front. Talk about a low life neighbourhood and run down building," said Woody. He flipped a switch to elevate the broadcast antenna. "Got your tape loaded? Batteries OK?"

"Just you worry about getting your story, my main man," said Punky, with a placid smile and a purr. She took a joint from her bag and added, "How much time do you think we have?"

"We have to do this *ASAP* to go live on the next newscast. The timing has to be perfect. The studio is expecting us to cut in at two minutes past the hour. Neville thinks we're going to be at the *Götterdämmerung Seniors' Home* to do that story on how a bunch of old Krauts re-use their adult incontinence diapers. Neville probably wears them too. It's about time I—we—showed that old fossil we can break the biggest story of the week. Maybe then he'll treat me with the respect I deserve."

"So, what you're saying is, I don't have enough time for a little reefer madness. Bummm-merrr."

Woody looked at his watch, and said, "I want to surprise this guy if I can, and maybe I can make him angry enough to blurt out a few things about the plagues and what was going down on Kubrick Island. If he was there, he must know something and I'm going to squeeze it out of him."

"Woody-he-man the aggressor, I love it," said Punky, fingering and smelling her joint. She looked in the side mirror and said, "Hey, Wood-burger, check out the geeks behind us."

Woody turned to see two Asian men in their twenties, sandpaper short hair, with horn-rimmed glasses, a ludicrous amount of bling, and hip-hop shorts hanging low. They stood in quiet conversation beside their Smart Car.

"Black horn-rims are a nice nerdy touch to go with—wait! Over there by the entrance—that's got to be him with the blonde. This is perfect—go go go!" shouted Woody, bolting from the car with a cordless mike in hand. Punky stowed the joint behind her ear and scrambled out, heaving the video camera onto her shoulder.

Lou and Tanya snaked across the sidewalk. "Sorry, pardon me, excuse me," said Lou, edging through the crowd.

Woody forced his way through the skateboarders, and spoke into his microphone while reaching out to Lou with his left hand. "Woody Logan, live on ECO TV with the ECO TV News Team of top-notch investigative reporters. Sir, can we talk to you on TV?"

Lou glanced at the young dweeb briefly, his lips wrinkled shut. He pulled his hat over his eyes and shook his head.

"Sir, there's been another outbreak of plague! Can you tell me about the most recent outbreak of disease at Kubrick Island?" said Woody, trying to step in front of Lou and Tanya.

Some of the skateboarding teenagers started to form a crowd around Woody and Punky, mugging for the camera.

"A confidential source identified you! Is it true your private plane was on Kubrick Island yesterday? A luxurious, private corporation jet airplane registered to *GLUM Experts*?"

"*Scusa, signore, no parla l'inglese,*" muttered Lou in a high-pitched gravelly voice, as he and Tanya forced their way toward the street corner and the safety of his car. As Woody turned to follow, the two Asian men got into the Smart Car. The teenagers were now pushing each other, fighting for a spot in front of the camera.

Woody began to realize the day was lost, and that this was not merely another monumentally bad idea but could spell the end of his career. In a panic he tried to salvage the situation.

"The Bahamian authorities identified the jet. How are you involved? Do you deny responsibility? How are you involved in all this?" he shouted at the side window of Lou's old Volkswagen as it pulled away from the curb.

Woody's insides went from panic to terror, and in a moment of dissociation he lost his focus and became absorbed by the curtained van, which was beginning a rhythmic, rocking motion with accompanying squeaks and howls from the interior. He pictured himself as a happy-go-lucky ne'er do well, having the time of his life inside the van with a bottle of wine and that cute redheaded girl from his high school who never would go out with him, instead of his current bowel churning and twisting terror. One of the teens shouted, "When this van's rockin' don't come knockin'!" to the puerile delight of his gang. This snapped Woody out of his trance and back to his broadcast.

"Sadly, yet another overpaid, multi-millionaire corporate tycoon has denied responsibility and shirked his ethical duty to the press and to the public's right to know everything about everyone all the time. Meanwhile, the plagues continue mercilessly." Woody watched helplessly as Punky shifted the camera lens to a wider angle and did a panoramic shot of the crowd, and over toward the van. He tried to follow to keep himself onscreen, only to see the van rocking faster and faster, and the teens mimicking it with rutting noises and pelvic thrusting motions at each other.

Woody shouted over their raucous laughter and grunting, "Thank heavens, so far the infections have been confined to isolated areas with very small populations. If the next epidemic were to strike a modern metropolis such as New York or Beijing, can you imagine the magnitude of the catastrophe?"

The teens seemed to find this funny, and began laughing and shouted, "You're a TV catastrophe, wiener!" "Skinny nerd!" "Loser." "Geek!" Fortunately the last few words were drowned out by various animal noises and more laughter as some of the teens returned to mock humping.

Woody slowed to a feeble finish. ". . . millions, billions of precious lives at stake, innocent people just like these precious, vivacious, youngsters in this neighbourhood. The humanity, oh, the humanity. This is Woody Logan for ECO TV News."

Punky gave the "off the air" signal with a finger across her throat, stuck her tongue out and added a mock suicide by hanging gesture. "*Aaargh!* Sorry Woody, but that was one big stinker of a story. Biggest *SNAFU* ever and you insisted we go unauthorized on live TV."

"Neville's going to kill me. I'm finished in this business."

"Time to start looking for another job. Why don't you start by asking those delivery guys if they need another driver?"

"Huh?"

Woody turned to see a large, black, delivery van with darkened windows slowly pull out into traffic, headed in the same direction as Lou.

Mr. Park stepped from the tour bus, followed by the seven other members of his team. He allowed himself a few seconds to enjoy the warm Cuban sun, then took a plastic pitch pipe from his shirt pocket and blew a soft C-sharp.

With a conductor's hand wave from Mr. Park, the group began to hum softly the opening bars of *The Battle Hymn of the Republic*. When the humming reached the first chorus, Mr. Park pointed toward the Zapata clinic, and they began a *pimp roll* march through the double doors.

A large security guard rose from his chair, but before he could speak his larynx was crushed by a fatal side kick by Mr. Ping. Mr. Pun courteously assisted the guard back into his chair for one final expiration before his throat swelled completely shut. Neither chorister missed a beat.

The humming octet halted at the open office door of Dr. Garcia Montez, who was finishing stitching the lacerated hand and forearm of a patient. The humming finally attracted Garcia's attention. He looked up at the group of eight young Asian men with horn-rimmed glasses, Hip Hop attire, and automatic pistols. They smiled and nodded in unison, and kept humming.

"Nice tune you are humming, boys," said Montez, "Are you part of the choir?"

"You are too kind, sir. We are merely a glee club," said Mr. Park. "Dr. Montez, I assume?"

Montez nodded slowly, eyes darting to the exit.

"And you, sir, are you Mr. Luigi Gubriace? Lou? From Toronto?" said Mr. Park, eyes locked on the patient, fingering his pistol.

"Who, me? No, no, the name is Stu, not Lou, Stu Guccione from Montreal. Stu's the name, life insurance is the game. I don't know any Lou."

Mr. Park drew his pistol and the rest of his team followed. "Close enough," he said, and the little clinic erupted in automatic gunfire.

A few minutes later, the tour bus pulled away from the clinic to a safe distance. Mr. Po pressed a button on his cell phone and the clinic exploded in flames. The choral humming resumed.

"Sorry, my mistake," shouted Lou as a brand spanking new, cherry red convertible cut in front of his rusty, ear-wax orange 1957 Volkswagen Beetle. The transmission gave out a grinding noise as Lou changed gears with the manual stick shift.

"Lou, please to keep mind on getting us to FPS office, ignore young man with bright red ego," said Tanya, eyes locked on her computer.

"Traffic is brutal. We might be faster walking," said Lou, hunched over the steering wheel.

"Is now high time for city widen road, give more room for cars."

"Tanya, that is just so environmentally wrong. Did I ever tell you my theory of—"

"Sorry mention sensitive issues of automobiles. Please let environment take care of itself for now and we finish job at hand."

"Finish the job, I wish we could. I feel like a total failure. All I've managed to do so far is to get sick, nearly die, and blow the best chance we had at Kubrick. Now we've got some preppy journalist and his little punk rock videographer trying to pin something on us."

"Not now worry about preppy young man with nice tight buttock muscles, he is not following," said Tanya, glancing at the side mirror. She pulled a makeup mirror from her purse and took a surreptitious look behind. "Maybe worry about little Smart Car who is following us, now two cars back, since leaving office. Two young men. Look like all day play many video games."

"Just a coincidence, I'm sure. We've only gone a couple of miles and a lot of traffic takes this route. There, look, they just turned off." Lou glanced back in the rear view mirror a few times, to reassure himself.

"Not that it matters. It's only a matter of time before nature hits us with a serious plague. For decades, we've been overdue for an utterly, monstrously bad pandemic that could wipe out billions of people. Maybe this thing is a natural bug, after all. It's increasingly likely with the environmental catastrophes mounting. Did you know that one of the most deadly viruses, Ebola, mutated to an airborne strain right in a lab? The next one is sure to kill us all. Ebola can do to a human body in 10 days what it takes AIDS 10 years to accomplish. Horrible way to die, Ebola. Viral hemorrhagic fever. You may not be aware of it at first, but your immune system fails soon after you are infected. Then there is blood in your sputum, and soon all your tissues start bleeding. You trickle blood from nearly every pore in your body, your eyes, your nose, your ears, your mouth, all of your gums start to bleed, then your whole alimentary canal starts bleeding."

"Lou, I have heard enough please. Is too much information." Tanya reached for a CD and plunked it into the car's stereo.

"Wait, this is only the first part. Then blood starts to leak from your rear, and you think you've lost control over your bowels. But you haven't lost control in the usual sense. You don't understand what's happening in your own body, due to the unimaginably excruciating pain and high fever, sometimes with delirium, but then you finally start to throw up stuff that looks like a mixture of raw hamburger, coffee grounds and carrot chowder, and then, and only then, does it dawn on you that this nasty little virus is slowly dissolving all of your insides, and everything in you is turning into some sort of organ soup."

"Lou! I am almost losing lunch in your car. Can you please for once to try to be in state of denial, like polite, normal human person, *da?"* Tanya turned up the stereo to the maximum volume as Prokofiev's *Troika* blasted from the speakers. "Like Lou more when he is sounding like Hamlet."

"But that's not the worst. Maybe organ soup or chowder is not exactly the right phrase, maybe organ stew, or organ chilli is more descriptive. Some of your insides aren't completely dissolved before you throw them up, so you get all this chunky stuff mixed in with the bloody hamburger meat and coffee grounds. Mother Nature is truly amazing, sometimes, isn't she, how she cares for all her little ones like us? Like the shepherd and the lost sheep? All part of some vast, eternal, divine plan. What do you think, Tanya, does it sound more like organ soup, stew, or chilli? . . . Tanya? . . . . Can you hear me over the stereo, Tanya?"

The two seater, electric Smart Car pulled into a laneway off a side street and parked between two dilapidated wooden garages. The driver, Mr. Yang, stepped out first, followed by Mr. Yen.

"Mr. Yen, this will not do. Look at yourself, you, you *non compos mentis* mooncalf. You bring shame upon me, your teacher. If you expect to blend in with the population, you must dress in the same absurd yet fashionable manner as trendy young men in North America."

"But, Mr. Yang, I have on the specified garments, the oversized, short-length trousers suspended from white boxer shorts, the latest untied sneakers two sizes too large with colour-coded laces, and an ostentatious display of bling. Is my bling out of date already?"

"Your hat, Mr. Yen, is a deerstalker cap, more appropriate to the 19th than the 21st century. Better to leave it behind in our vehicle or donate it to a museum than to wear it so conspicuously. And your weapon, always hide it in the backside of your shorts."

Mr. Yen stowed his hat in the car and slid his automatic pistol to the rear of his shorts.

"Much better. Now, assume a sneering expression indicating a contemptuous attitude to authorities and to your elders."

Mr. Yen curled his upper lip to the left, turned his head to an angle to display flared nostrils.

"Splendid, Mr. Yen. The slouching posture is well done. We may now commence the *pimp roll*. Walk this way, if you please."

Mr. Yang assumed a bow legged stance and began an ambling, bouncing, affected gait that gave the impression of swinging a large, pendulous mass somewhere deep inside his shorts. Mr. Yen struggled to maintain the *pimp roll* and the slouch at the same time. He sneered at a nearby nun and priest, baring his teeth for good measure.

"Excellent, Mr. Yen. Now, no one will notice us as we approach our targets."

A few minutes and one lost lunch later, Lou and Tanya parked the Volkswagen at a corner and started to push their way through the pedestrian crowds toward the FPS office, one long block away, up a moderately steep hill.

"Sorry, pardon me, oops!" muttered Lou as pedestrians continually bumped into him. "All my fault, sorry, I beg your pardon, excuse me, my bad, man."

"Lou, knock it off. You are not in Canada."

Tanya's cell phone rang with a *Troika*. She held her computer with one hand and pulled out her cell phone from her jacket pocket with the other. "*Da* . . . Yes . . . I understand . . . just now? And all of them! . . . Who? . . . why . . . Holy snapping turtles. OK. *Da svidanya.*"

"Sorry, my mistake, pardon me—"

"Lou! Listen, is very important. Russian friend in Cuban embassy has very bad news. Zapata Clinic is now bombed. All dead."

"Dr. Montez? Garcia?"

"All of them gone. Lou, there was patient this morning look like you, kind of Italian man, but not very much macho, not like Marcello, or Giancarlo . . . sorry, nice looking man. Maybe they think they killed you."

"The samples—did they get the samples to Winnipeg?"

"*Nyet*. Was courier for lab who first on scene and find mess. All destroyed in explosion, samples, records, everything lost. Cuban police suspect some sort of funny looking tour group in area, maybe Korean Glee Club."

"Let's get to that FPS guy fast. Joe and Jill should be just a few minutes behind us by now."

Lou and Tanya moved as fast as they could through the crowds without drawing undue attention. They dodged a number of beggars and buskers, including a rotund, Slavic looking man with a handlebar moustache, playing *Troika* on his accordion and dancing like an arthritic and morose circus bear. Tanya scanned the street numbers. "219 is electronics store, so number 221 is—"

"Too late," said Lou, looking in disgust at the burned out and boarded up shell of the former FPS shipping office. "We're always one step behind."

Tanya pulled Lou's sleeve toward the window of the electronics store, and whispered, "Do not look directly, Lou, watch reflection in glass. Across street, those two Asian mens in ludicrous clothes, looks like clown suits. Shorter one may have congenital facial deformity. I think same ones in Smart Car following us."

"I can't quite see them for the chubby accordion player," Lou began. He was interrupted by a quiet "*pffft!*" and a small drop of blood spattered the window in front of him. The accordion wheezed out its last *Troika,* and the morose accordionist collapsed on the sidewalk a few feet away. Pedestrians simply stepped around him, with a few mutterings about drunken beggars cluttering the sidewalk.

Lou and Tanya ducked into the doorway of the electronics store. A TV in the window showed the interview with Karl and Cookie, now in a three way group hug, with the Bonobo making pelvic thrusts at Cookie's breasts.

"They've disappeared, probably behind the garbage truck across the street," said Lou, *sotto voce*. "After the Zapata business it's clear they're after me, not you. Find the security guard in here and stick to him."

"I can look after myself," said Tanya, umbrage in her voice.

"Of course you can, but I need you to call Joe on your cell. Tell him I'm going to try to lead these clowns back toward the Volkswagen. We need to question them, and we absolutely need to keep these guys alive."

Tanya nodded and Lou stepped onto the sidewalk. A small crowd had now gathered around the accordion player, which provided some cover for Lou. A group of teenagers with "Eco Angels" t-shirts were moving downhill, and Lou slipped into step with them. He started an inane conversation about their "neat" and "cool" t-shirts, and what groovy hep cats the Eco Angels were for doing all that swell environmental stuff, all the while looking alternately ahead toward the Volkswagen and behind in the direction of his pursuers.

Soon Lou stood on the street corner, putting the Volkswagen between him and his would be assassins, oblivious to the black delivery van approaching. He took a good look up the street, and saw the two Hip Hop boys cautiously emerge from behind the garbage truck and work their way downhill, apparently trying to blend in with the crowd by doing the *pimp roll*. Further up the street a large Hummer, possibly Joe's, came to a stop.

What happened next caused Lou to stop breathing for almost a minute. Tanya casually left the electronics store, white laptop in hand. She adopted the gait of an office worker on her way home, walked directly behind the nearest assassin, and with an ear shattering *Kiai!* crashed her laptop onto his occipital lobe with all her strength.

The would-be assassin was clearly knocked unconscious, with no dramatic Hollywood tumbling or pratfall, just a look of complete relaxation, as the shoulders gave up their tension, the eyes closed, the jaw dropped, the knees folded, and the rest followed into a flaccid heap.

The second assassin was taken by surprise, but had a split second to defend himself. Tanya caught him with an uppercut *swack* with her laptop, which he partially blocked with his shoulder. She threw a fast front kick into the groin, doubling him over, and finished him off with another glancing blow to the head with her now battered laptop.

Lou saw Joe, pistol in hand, rush from the Hummer toward Tanya, followed by Jill. Then Joe started pointing in Lou's direction, and shouted, loud enough to be heard a block away, "Behind you! LOU!"

Only then did Lou notice the large black delivery van approaching him, its sliding door agape. The last thing he saw was all three of his partners pointing in his direction, and then a black hood went over his head. He could feel four massive hands grasp him by the arms and shoulders and heave him effortlessly onto the van's floor, holding him down.

The van's sliding door closed with a *crunch*, and Lou felt a surge of acceleration. Another passenger crouched down beside him, his garlic breath almost palpable from inside the hood.

Then he clearly heard the deep, menacing whisper in his left ear.

"You have no idea, no idea at all, the trouble you are in now . . . Luigi."

"I know that voice!"

CHAPTER 4

Where's Lou?

Dressed in a set of green surgical scrubs, with a surgical mask hanging loosely from her neck, Jill slowly unpacked the contents of yet another package of her specialized equipment onto a long table. She kept an eye on the other occupants of the "Royal Suite," a windowless concrete bunker that might have once been an underground garage. There were no visual or auditory clues to the location, merely a supply of water, light, electricity, and an industrial size floor drain. A large steel door with a padlocked bolt was the only exit.

In one corner, the comatose body of Mr. Yen lay handcuffed to a water pipe, shallow breathing the only evidence of life. His partner and would-be fellow assassin, Mr. Yang, sat on a steel chair beneath a bare light bulb, with a good view of the floor drain. Joe finished tightening the ropes securing him to the chair.

"OW! That's too tight—let me go, you bloody gargantuan fecalith!" exclaimed Yang.

Joe easily hoisted the chair and Yang overhead, upside down. "What did I tell you? No foul language, please. It's not nice to be impolite."

As the inverted Yang contemplated his options, Tanya casually walked up and softly whispered into Yang's ear, "I suggest it may be good idea apologize to nice large man, *da?*"

"Sorry sir, very sorry indeed, utterly rude of me to use such an inappropriate scatological term. I abjectly and humbly apologize. I am truly sorry and completely and utterly contrite," said Yang, unable to control his saliva while verbally grovelling from the position he found himself in.

Joe sat him down gently, and said to Tanya, "He said he was sorry."

Jill finished arranging a neat series of white towels over her supplies, not allowing Yang to see clearly what was in store for him.

"I think we're just about ready for you, Mr. Yang. It is Mr. Yang, is it not?" she said.

"I'm not afraid of you, you paramedic manqué, you f—," he began, stopping himself as Joe raised an eyebrow. "Let me rephrase that. I respectfully suggest that intimidation of any sort will be utterly fruitless. May I add that I am completely impervious to physical pain, and fully trained to resist psychological torture. Furthermore—"

He stopped when Jill picked up a saw-toothed clamp from the table and waved it in his direction. "I think we've got a bad case of logorrhoea. Are you ready to answer a few questions, Mr. Yang?"

"Mmm-mmm," said Yang, shaking his head for *No*.

"Perhaps, you can begin by telling us who you are working for, and why he sent you, and your somnolent partner, to kill an innocent man," said Jill, replacing the clamp on the table. "Please."

"Ha! If you knew, you would be begging me for mercy. He has agents everywhere. Even now, our people are looking for me with diligence, and it is only a matter of time before our positions are reversed, and it will be I asking questions of exceeding impertinence." He glanced toward Joe, who was busy examining the door bolt, turned back to Jill and added in a whisper, "*Dai bei!* Big nose!"

"Well now, we must make the best possible use of our time." Jill pulled a latex glove onto her left hand. "I think we should become better acquainted." She turned her back to Yang and began fiddling with something as she continued. "Let me begin by telling you that I am a doctor, with an advanced specialty in forensic psychiatry, well acquainted with a criminal mind such as yours."

She turned around, adjusting the latex fingers on her right hand, and slowly unrolled a veterinarian's bovine obstetrical glove, which reached up to the shoulder of her small frame, a slight smile betraying her sadistic delight.

"I have a number of professional interests. The nerves which control the sensation of pain, for example." She looked directly into Yang's eyes, pulling his eyelids wide open. "I did a detailed study of the pain transmitting nerves of the face. The trigeminal nerve, for example," she said, stroking his cheek, "which you may have become aware of if you had a severe toothache, or root canal surgery on your upper wisdom teeth, can only be properly dissected if the patient is fully conscious. There are some very amusing drugs which can amplify the painful sensations considerably. Have you any masochistic tendencies, Mr. Yang?"

"No, doctor, but thank you for asking," said Yang, with considerably less confidence in his voice.

"Pity, it might have amused me. But we shall leave your face intact a while longer, and give you something else to contemplate. In some other areas, I am considered more of a talented amateur than a professional. For example, I've considered doing a speculative paper on the highly effective techniques of interrogation via proctology."

Jill retrieved an instrument from her table, held it behind her back, and stared at Yang from less than a foot away.

"So without further delay," she said, holding a gleaming, chromium-steel speculum in front of Yang's eyes. "Who are you working for?"

She snapped the speculum wide open with a metallic *clang!* "And tell us, please, where have they taken Lou?"

Karl Mendel's mountain lair was a private château which lay in an isolated area high in the French Alps, a short distance from Switzerland. A few hundred metres down the only access road was the modern *Mendel Research Laboratories* building. The two main structures were separated by a large hill and several hectares of mature coniferous forest, contiguous with the forested valley leading to the unguarded border. A number of smaller structures maintained a respectable distance from the Mendel residence and gardens, all within an easy walk to the laboratories. Gardeners tended the landscaping, floral and vegetable gardens, which included a centrepiece floral sundial, whose blooms now indicated the end of the day was approaching.

The château itself dated from the days of the *ancien régime*, with recent renovations adding the finest of modern luxuries and technological enhancements without detracting from the original architecture. An astronomical observatory, several chimneys and turrets dominated the outline of the roof. On the largest turret lay an object several metres in length, covered by a tarpaulin with a camouflage pattern.

In what was once a family chapel, shafts of sunlight streamed through the stained glass windows and onto the stone columns and marble floor. Karl Mendel, the great hope of the global environmental movement, sat at his pipe organ, lovingly performing his own interpretation of Bach's *Toccata and Fugue in D minor*. His performance was rich and forceful, but he had not yet pulled out all the stops.

The last few notes slowly died out, echoing among the hard reflecting surfaces, as DeWang stood at attention respectfully in the doorway, his nose pointed upward. Only when Karl looked up from the keyboards did DeWang approach, point to his watch, and gesture toward the hallway.

"Excellent timing, DeWang," said Karl, checking the hands on the antique, three metre tall, rococo-style grandfather clock. The clock provided a visual counterpoint to the organ, separated by several intricately carved wooden panels illustrating the seven deadly sins. The cardinal virtues were not to be found in this home.

"We mustn't keep you-know-who waiting," said Karl.

"The others are in the library, sir, if you please." DeWang gave a short bow and preceded his employer through the hallway, around the base of the grand staircase, past a small lecture hall, and opened the library door for him.

Karl's library held over 20,000 volumes, mainly of historical and aesthetic value. Flat-panel screens, computers, and monitors were unobtrusively housed in custom-made cabinets of prime growth teak, mahogany and other rare woods. The room was dominated by a wooden conference table, a polished cross-sectional slice of a giant California redwood, bare except for a single speaker-phone at the centre. In a shadowed corner, an elderly male figure sat in an electric wheelchair, smoking a marijuana cigarette beside an open window, and emitting the occasional guttural moan.

Mei Tung Nga still had the power to take Karl's breath away at times, even after their seven years of intimate relations. There was something about the traditional Chinese silk slit skirt, her legs crossed just so, the twirl of her ankle, and the toss of her long black hair that commanded Karl's attention this morning. Mei sat at the table holding a fading volume entitled *Jane Austen ~ Letters*. She looked up and said "Karl, you must listen to this. 'How horrible it is to have so many people killed!—And what a blessing that one cares for none of them!' Isn't that just a perfect sentiment?"

"Splendid, my learned lovely, and so apropos to the occasion," said Karl, stroking her long, black hair gently, his hormone flurry subsiding. "But try to keep the discussion to a rudimentary level for our sponsor. Generations of inbreeding do have drawbacks, O cerebral siren of my cortex."

"Karl, do I have to be here for this? The man's a complete moron."

"I understand, multi-talented muse of my mind. He is, indeed, so phenomenally stupid he doesn't even know how stupid he is."

"He's such an arrogant, big eared donkey! I can't stand the snob, and I don't care about how much money he has or who he knows."

"Ah, but that big fat chequebook and all those connections will make our future together possibly perfect, radiant light of my life. And I think he likes you. It's only for a little while longer, and then—"

Karl was interrupted by a signal from his communications system, the first bar of Beethoven's *Fifth Symphony.* A large screen monitor emerged from a sequoia wood-panelled cabinet, and Karl pushed a button on the speaker-phone. An image formed on the screen, a middle aged Anglo-Saxon man, with a quasi military blazer, greying hair, and surrounded by a luxurious apartment. He bore an uncanny resemblance to a well known branch of European monarchy.

"Welcome, Your Royal Highness," Karl began. "I believe you know my most trusted confidante, Mei Tung Nga. The Professor will join us momentarily."

"No need for formality here, Karl, all friends, teammates so to speak. Mei, please call me 'Monty.' But only in private, of course."

"Most kind of you, Monty," she said with a well rehearsed smile, digging a fingernail into her book.

Aaaaaaacccchh! came a moan from the shadowy corner. Karl and Mei blinked in unison and smiled a little harder.

"Karl, the latest transfer of funds, all hunky-dory, I trust? All safe from prying eyes?"

"Yes, thank you so much, Monty. It was all completely clandestine, with no trail back to Your Royal—to yourself. Very generous of you, and the funds will be put to the best possible use."

"Seems overly complicated, all this stuff and nonsense. Couldn't we just set off a few thousand H-bombs, deal with the stinking, unwashed masses in that way? Be done with all the filthy slopes and colonial sausage jockeys in one go?" Monty refilled his porcelain teacup from a silver urn.

"Very good idea, Monty, but it does lead to some sticky complications. Radiation gets around a bit, could affect the wrong people, might even affect your horses."

"I see, can't have that. Took me ages to breed a brace of polo ponies worth keeping. Very well, Karl, we shall carry on with your plan. Were the tests successful?"

"Completely perfect! Perhaps Professor Pfizz could give us the latest statistics."

Professor Erik Pfizz tossed the stub of his reefer out the window and pushed the control stick on his electric wheelchair, emerged from the shadows and parked beside the table. "Ohh, *die Hände in den Schoß legen*, nothing like it for releasing the tension there is. *Mein Herr*, you practice regularly?"

"Not now, Professor," said Karl with a toothy smile toward Monty. "The latest experimental statistics? Hmm?"

"We have had the perfect results on the Island of Strom-boli. Precisely as predicted, there were 40 dead, no more, no less. A few more tests for the statistical con-fidence and the final results will be within our control completely. We will tolerate NO ERRORS!" said Erik with a thump of his fist on the table.

"Good news, I dare say, Professor. I am sure all the icky-techy stuff is well taken care of. But Karl, my valet showed me a disturbing little bit of TV news, some odd berk seems to have gotten wind of the business on Kubrick prematurely. Chasing some *I-tie* looking chap he was, you know, a dago, Loobey Goobey something or other. Some sort of *wop* name."

Mei held her book in front of her right hand, the middle finger extended. Karl gave her a sweet smile and she smiled at the screen with her lips, while her eyes narrowed to razor-thin slits.

"I know who you mean, an odious little chap, known as Lou Gubrious."

"He probably reeks of unwashed perspiration and garlic," added Monty.

"But not for long, I can assure you. At this very moment, my best people are taking care of Mr. Gubrious," said Karl.

"We should also deal with the scruffy, impudent, young Yankee journalist who broke the story."

"Another splendid idea, Monty. In fact, I think we can arrange a special and most fitting end for the nosy newsman can't we, Professor?"

"Mmmm. *Ja*. We can help him play the main role in the very interesting scientific experiment, which will not be repeated." Erik started to chuckle but soon coughed up some phlegm.

"All is well in hand, then, Karl. The only other thing I could ask is that you could knock off a few dozen royals at the same time, bring me closer to the big job, what?"

"Perhaps in the cleanup phase, deal with a few loose ends, eh what?" said Karl to the screen with a wink.

"Please do so, Karl. All righty, cheery bye, all."

"Cheery-bye, Monty," said Karl, clicking the off switch. The image of Monty with his golden-braided uniform and china teacup dissolved to black.

Mei swatted Karl on the shoulder with her book, and gave him an icy glare. "If you start talking like that inbred, illiterate, racist, polo-playing PIG I swear I will vivisect you. Slowly. Starting with your tongue."

"Must keep our wealthy benefactor jollied along for now, eh wh—shouldn't we, my love goddess?"

Mei's expression softened a bit.

"My one and only true soul mate? Eve to my Adam?" he said, tickling her in the rib.

Mei surrendered with a giggle, and Karl relaxed, secure in the knowledge that she could be kept in her place with a little romantic hyperbole and vague hints of the possible chance of some sort of potential partnership, slightly resembling an ill-defined and loose form of something like commitment at some unspecified time in the distant future, without his being so foolish as to clearly commit to anything.

"Mei, perhaps you and the Professor can think of an appropriate end for him, for the good of the planet, a touch of poetic justice, hmmm?"

Erik's eyes betrayed a sadistic glint. "Another idea for dealing with such a *dummkopf* I have. Perhaps the long, detailed, lec-ture, sparing no technical details of my research, I think. Maybe I will be having this time a new world rec-ord for the longest lec-ture."

"Will that be enough to finish him off?" said Mei.

"If he the lec-ture survives, then for sure the glass booth, *ja*?" Erik gave a little self satisfied chuckle.

"What a wonderful sendoff, Professor, and we could all enjoy another of your very thorough presentations. But we may have to move quickly between now and the big day," said Karl.

Mei went into a pout. "All right, but tell me it's only a matter of a few days."

"Mere hours, my houri of Paradise." Karl's demeanour shifted to sour, and he began pacing. "There's only one little thing bothering me. I withheld a bit of news from his royal idiocy for simplicity."

"*Was?*" said Erik.

"Mr. Lou Gubrious vanished before the Hip Hop boys finished their work. Everything was going perfectly, but no one on earth seems to be able to answer a simple question: *Where is Lou?*"

Jill carefully inserted the tip of a hypodermic syringe into a vial of clear liquid, filled it to the maximum 30 ml mark, withdrew it, and gave it a few taps and a squirt to remove any air bubbles. Tanya watched her nervously, while Joe kept an eye on Yang's unconscious partner, Yen.

Jill turned to Yang with her best bedside manner smile. "You talk a lot Mr. Yang but you haven't told us anything we want to know."

"I told you I know nothing! I am totally ignorant, uninformed, unenlightened and completely in the dark of such details. The comatose Mr. Yen communicated with our employer, and now he can tell us nothing, thanks to your overly zealous, pugilistic colleague."

Jill approached him with the hypodermic in hand. "Would you like us to use a chemical method of persuasion? I have a delicious witches' brew of sodium thiopental, amobarbital, scopolamine, and just a pinch of Dr. Jill's secret recipe of sugar and spice and everything nice. We can start you off with 5 ml, and there's lots more here if we need it. I'm told it actually feels rather pleasant, in small doses, a euphoric sensation with just enough stimulation to keep your tongue moving. Within a few minutes you will cheerfully tell us your most intimate thoughts and feelings, all your secrets, babbling on and on like a gossiping schoolgirl. You will trust me with everything."

"I thought you were going to use that other thing to squeeze and knead it out of me."

"The danger with the mechanical approach is that you might only tell us what you think we want to hear in order to make us stop. But why don't we let you choose which way to go. I could use the speculum and some other instruments that could prove effective.

Or a little poke of a needle and a nice, warm and fuzzy feeling. What shall it be, Mr. Yang, the needle or the speculum? Make your choice: tick-tock," she said, snapping the speculum open and shut in tick-tock time.

Yang glanced at the chromium steel implement of aperture enlargement and quickly said, "The needle will do just fine, thank you."

"That's what we were waiting for, the first sign of compliance. Now it's all downhill. Much easier to flow with the eternal Tao, Mr. Yang." Jill pulled up his sleeve and rubbed his arm with an alcohol swab. "Any history of diabetes, hypoglycaemia, hernia, herpes, haemorrhoids, heart disease, schizophrenia, epilepsy? Not planning on driving a motor vehicle or operating heavy equipment in the next 24 hours?"

Yang shook his head "No" and looked away with his face scrunched up.

"It is *so* nice to know you are completely impervious to physical pain. Just a teensy fear of doctors and needles, is it?" said Jill. "Be absolutely still now, it's very important that you do not move."

She probed his left shoulder and biceps area carefully before choosing the exact spot for insertion. The first few millimetres of penetration were without incident. Then Yang let out a horrific "*Aaarrrggghhh!!!*" and rocked the chair back. Jill caught him with her free hand to prevent him from falling; Yang resisted, and in the struggle the plunger of the hypodermic went all the way in.

"Oh, no!" she shouted. "He jumped and the whole 30 ml went directly into his brachial vein all at once. In seconds it will hit his brain!"

"You trying kill him?" shouted Tanya. She looked to Joe, who shrugged helplessly.

"It was a mistake—I told him to hold still," Jill exclaimed. She appeared to be on the verge of tears, and in a panic checked Yang's eyes, and took his pulse.

Yang's head drooped slightly, a stalactite shaped drool of saliva forming. He then jerked his head upwards, eyes wide open, pupils dilated. "Ohhh, wow! That so gooooood! You beautiful lady doctor, nice firm, round canteloupe boobs, you all such nice people. I never noticed how beautiful you all are in this wonderful little room. Even big fecalith man is attractive, in platonic sort of way. I feel, I feel funny, maybe wet myself. Oops! Number two. Good night, big mama with beautiful butt when bending over, sleep now, thank you for, for . . . whatever." Yang mumbled something in Cantonese before passing into a coma.

Jill quickly took his blood pressure. "60 over 35, dropping, pulse slowing, respiration shallow."

Tanya shouted, "Do something—give antidote, stimulant, anything!"

"Nothing short of a heart and lung machine can save him," said Jill. She shone the beam of a small flashlight into his eyes, and simply said "Gone."

Tanya's face turned the colour of borscht. She picked up her black backup laptop computer with both hands and slowly walked toward Jill with a look that could kill.

Joe was bent over the body of Yen. He looked up and shouted "Whoa, Tanya. This guy's dead too. You killed him."

"We had two potential leads, and we kill one each," said Tanya, lowering her computer and relaxing her face a notch.

Joe looked around the Royal Suite. "Now we got no leads, and no Lou."

Yang's bodily fluids oozed toward the floor drain with an eerie, trickling sound.

❦

Woody stood on his left foot at the phone booth, polishing the toe of his right foot against his trouser leg, holding the phone with one hand and his Eco-bike with the other.

He glanced at the homeless bag ladies, winos, and professional beggars in the park, thinking he would soon join them. Maybe he could pretend to be blind, so he could eke out a living as a beggar. Maybe he could just jump off the nearest bridge.

"No sir, absolutely no excuse whatsoever, utter stupidity on my part." He polished the other toe, not that that would help, even if his boss could inspect him.

"You thundering, blundering, dunderhead! A mistake a first year journalism student wouldn't make." Neville's voice boomed over the phone from his office several blocks away, at a decibel level that made the telephone system almost superfluous. "You did this entirely without approval, and the blame rests solely upon you. *NOW* do you understand why we have policies and procedures? Rules of the game, if that makes it easier for a nincompoop like you to understand?"

"Yes sir, I should have reviewed the company manual more often," said Woody. An oblate spheroid of an accordion player strolled by, playing *So long, fare thee well, adios, it's over*. In his terror, Woody had another momentary spell of dissociation, and pictured himself with an unkempt beard, taking up the banjo and becoming a tobacco chewing, moonshine chugging, bluegrass busker with a bevy of beautiful young bluegrass groupies craving his attention.

"And you can thank your videographer for distracting the viewers with a wide shot of all those idiot children regressing to their natural drooling ape behaviour and switching to an area wide microphone. With any luck most of the audience will think it was a story about school absenteeism with some audio problems."

"Yes sir, I must buy her some flowers, some candy, something to express my gratitude. Perhaps a new spiked dog collar."

"We've had quite enough levity from you, Logan, and not enough gravity."

"Gravity, yes sir. Perhaps my next assignment could be more within my capabilities, to demonstrate my utter, universal gravity and loyalty to the network," said Woody. If that was not enough grovelling, perhaps doing penance in the sports department would work. Neville Lear detested sports almost as much as abstract art.

"I would terminate your employment right now, if I could get it past Human Resources, but that would let you off the hook too easily. If I had my way you would be shipped off to an Inuit outpost to do environment stories at a nudist colony in the Canadian arctic in black fly season, so we could all watch you descend into the screaming madness of being eaten alive one milligram of worthless flesh at a time, and eventually die a slow and extremely painful death from exsanguination while babbling your illiterate, incompetent, mindless drivel to a local audience of brain dead solvent sniffers."

Woody held his breath, waiting for the axe to fall.

"However just that outcome may be, however much our loyal viewers might enjoy watching your overdue demise, it shall not happen, not yet. Karl Mendel, of all people, happened to see a video clip of your performance and for some incomprehensible reason he has taken a *liking* to you. It distresses me immensely to have to say it."

"*The* Karl Mendel?" Woody could not have been more surprised if Neville had said Santa Claus or the Pope. "He liked *me*?"

"He said you have some sort of a screen presence. More of a screen absence if I had my way. Now he wants you to host a global special from the ECO TV Paris studio."

"Who, *me*?"

"Probably wants you beside him to make him appear even more brilliant and attractive. He often uses developmentally delayed and deformed apes for that purpose, and that sub-human role may be barely within your pathetic capabilities."

"Global TV? With Karl Mendel? In the Paris studio? Next flight? I'm on it! I'm on it! But I still want to find out about this connection to this Gubriace guy."

"He can not have disappeared, you dunce. Almost a day later and you can't find him? Have you tried all your contacts?"

"Yes! And I still don't know where he is."

Unbeknownst to Woody, four Asian men with black horn rimmed glasses and Hip Hop attire sat in a four door stretch Mini Cooper, parked on the opposite side of the street with a good view of the phone booth.

Mr. Lee held a pair of binoculars in one hand and a cell phone in the other, and repeated one side of the conversation. ". . . Gogo teepee? With Karl Mendel? Into Paris stupido? Nix fight? I'm a nit! I'm a nit! But eyes still won't two fine doubts this conniption to dis Gooey Archie goy. . . . Yes, Auntie stole don't nowhere he is?"

His partners, Messrs Lei, Lie and Loh glanced at each other in puzzlement. Mr. Lei pointed to Woody as he mounted his Eco-bike and whispered "He's about to move."

Mr. Loh started the car as Mr. Lee continued his phone call. "Yes sir, precisely what he said. Nothing about a black van. No, I'm sure he doesn't know where Lou Gubrious is. Yes sir, immediately sir. The big Egyptian boxer and the Russian blonde. Absolutely. The outcome shall be indubitable at the earliest possible moment, and you shall be apprised immediately following the deed. Thank you sir."

Mr. Lee snapped his phone shut and turned to Mr. Loh. "Get moving. We have a new assignment. Gentlemen, check your pistols, we are going to spill blood."

Four automatic pistols clicked in unison as the stretch Mini Cooper pulled into traffic.

CHAPTER 5

Family is everything

The sprawling suburban home of Don Luciano Gubriace was designed in what the architect called a neo-Roman style, the entrance dominated by a quartet of two-storey, white marble Corinthian columns. An astute observer might look beyond the reproductions of classical Roman statues, the large gardens and orchards, the servants' quarters, the garages with a small fleet of European cars, and perhaps notice that today there were more gardeners than necessary, each with an automatic pistol in their overalls.

On this particular morning, a visitor pulling up to the house by way of the circular driveway would first have seen the large black delivery van parked to one side, incongruous with the rest of the residence. He might then have heard two deep male voices grunting, the sound coming from the basement.

Inside, two 400 pound twin brothers, Enrico and Mario, were engaged in a friendly sumo wrestling match. Mario reached for his brother's belt, leaving him just slightly off-balance. Enrico seized the opportunity to slide his right ankle behind his brother's left, and with a Herculean effort threw him just outside the circular border.

"Bravo, Enrico, bravo," shouted Luciano, "Today's grand-a champion."

"Bravo, Mario, too! You'll win next time," cheered their cousin Lucia, smiling with her trademark generous mouth that could snap up, in one bite, an entire cannoli, sideways.

"Hey Lou, how about a match? Best two out of three?" said Mario, crawling to his feet.

Lou contemplated the gravity of having Mario land on him with a cetacean belly flop and waved his hand to decline the offer. "You are too kind, Mario, but I'm more into word games, crosswords, chess, that type of thing."

Lou set aside his espresso and biscotti and turned to his host. "I really need to contact my team, Uncle Luciano. They must be wondering what happened to me."

"Hey, the family help you out plenty a-time," said Luciano with a stern, avuncular visage, "and now you gonna play my way, *capisce?*"

"I understand the need for secrecy but I do think it was a bit overly dramatic, the way you picked me up."

Luciano stroked his short grey beard and wagged a finger at his favourite nephew. "You listen to-a your uncle, all in good time. You're a good boy, Luigi, not like these two bums." He gave a smack on the back of the head to his son Enrico, who howled in mock agony, followed by a threatening wave to Mario, who covered his head in anticipation of a blow which never came.

"Look at these two good for nothings. All the time, they just party, they got no sense of *familglia*. I'm-a gonna be 67 soon, and no grandchildren yet. These goof-a-balls make me ashame. Not even married yet, and already they 27 years—"

"28, Papa!!" they shouted in unison.

"And my little niece, Lucia, look at those beautiful hips a yard wide and great big juicy milk jugs, I tell-a you Lou, she's built like a baby makin' machine."

"Uncle Luciano, *per favore!*"

64

"Already you too old for makin' the babies, what, you 30 something?"

"I'm 29!!"

"Yeah, you 29 for the ninth time. You 29 like I'm 39."

Lucia snapped up a newspaper, rolled it into a cylinder and whacked Don Luciano on the head.

"Ow! Hey, Lou, canna you see this beautiful girl pumpin' out the *bambini*, like the sausage outa you Uncle Franco's sausage machine in his butcher shop. *Ba-boom! Ba-boom! Ba-boom!* Now she's a bigga mama with triplets!!!"

Lucia gave him three whacks with the newspaper, and added a gentle whack for Lou, just to make him feel like part of the family. She then ran off to chase the twins.

"Luigi, *familglia* is everything. You gotta love life so much all you wanna do is make more of it, *capisce*? Why don' you marry that little Russian girl, make some little blond kids, eh?"

"Mmmm."

"Your Uncle Franco, he had 9 babies, now he's got 22 or 23 grand-a kids. Your great grandfather Luigi, back in the old country, you named for him, he had 12, 9 sons, 2 died, 3 daughters, 38 grandchildren, and I think now it's maybe 70 or 80 great grandchildren, somethin' like-a that."

"Hmm. Nice."

"Your *cugino*, Carmine, he's about your age and he's got 7, maybe 8 kids already, another on the way. Luigi, we gotta keep the numbers up, or the Sardinians gonna take over. Too many Sardinians. The Sardinians are the worst."

"Hmmmm. The way you put it, Uncle Luciano, it makes it seem like a global fertility competition."

"What you gonna do? Let the Muslims take over? You want the Chinese to run the world?"

"Just kidding. *Ha ha.* You know, Uncle Luciano, this could be the beginning of a great discussion, but if I could be allowed to make just one call, I—"

"Luigi, I gotta insist no phone calls, no nothing, until I say so. You gonna see why in a few minutes, I hope. Right now there's some of the worst-a bad guys inna the world who don't know what's goin' on, and that may buy us a little time. We got some serious stuff to talk about."

They were interrupted by the twins, who bellowed and thundered back into the family room with Lucia in hot pursuit. Luciano held up his hand and gave a short, sharp *Ssshhh!*

The room fell silent, and all five family members heard the sound of a vehicle parking in front of the house, and the main door upstairs opening. Luciano stood up to speak. "Luigi, that's the man we been-a waitin' for. Kids, we gonna talk about some real boring stuff, so maybe you young folks not gonna like it so much."

Lucia and the twins rolled their eyes in anticipation of a speech heard many times before.

"Here, boys, take something for a few snacks," said Luciano, handing them a wad of folding money. "Go down to the restaurant, have some pizzas, antipasti, secondi, maybe some nice cannoli for Lucia, eh? Take some more for drinks, and get some take-out food. You gotta keep your strength up, boys. Your cousin Luigi and me gonna talk about a lot of dull facts, try to figure out a few things, look at some maps and numbers, you wouldn't like it."

Enrico and Mario pocketed the cash and muttered a few grunts and grumbles of agreement.

"Don't worry, we gonna pick you up later with the van, and I'm promisin' you ain't-a gonna miss any of the real action," concluded Luciano.

"Unless you would like to talk about some abstract and theoretical environmental issues," said Lou, rubbing his hands in mock enthusiasm. "Maybe we could look at some hard scientific data and do some really neat mathematics, *hmm*?"

"Math?! *Yechhh!* That does it, we're out of here!" said Lucia, tugging on the boys' sleeves.

As soon as they were out the door, Luciano whispered to Lou, "Come up to the office. You gotta meet someone, a most special guy."

They took the spiral staircase to the main floor, then across a large dining room to the family office. Luciano looked around to make sure no other family members or servants lingered about. He opened the door and said "Luigi, do you remember your great uncle, Sergio? From *Firenze*?"

Lou's jaw dropped a full inch, and he managed to squeak out a *Si! Si!*

The spindly Sergio Spenalzo looked up from a computer, stood, and took his great nephew's shoulders into his arms, then gave him a light smack on the side of the head. "Hey, *cornuto!* You're in big trouble and you don't even know it." He hugged Lou and then smacked him again.

"I think I heard about that yesterday. I would love to hear more about it, Great Uncle Sergio."

Sergio took the dominant seat by the computer, and with a push of a button a large screen monitor popped on.

"So, your friend Brulé told you to go find out about these diseases, Mr. Big Shot Independent Investigator, and now you probably think maybe it's some *mezzo-fanook* fruitcake Muslim terrorist, or some drunken bum IRA bog trotter behind this, eh? Or maybe you think this is natural, the universe unfolding as it should." Sergio clicked the mouse and a world map appeared, showing the location of each outbreak and the number of victims. "Luigi, look at this."

Lou took a moment to carefully scan the screen. "Your map agrees with my data," said Lou. "So far there is nothing new."

The map faded to black and a maze of technical charts and numbers appeared on the screen. Sergio continued. "This is the best scientific data we have so far, and frankly, it stinks. Look at this."

"I think my colleague, Tanya Chekhov, found all of this yesterday. She hacked into the same sources. Sorry."

"Luigi, stop and think. The infectious species has not been identified after all these tests, and with all top notch scientists. Now that's very curious. *Why not?* I ask. So let's try another angle. The victims' autopsy results suggest that it's all likely the same organism, so let's take that as a postulate. Then we can look at the epidemiological data, and apply a little statistical analysis, and what we find—it's fantastic. All the outbreak locations are islands, and the epidemics affected only a relatively small part of the population, except for the few lost souls at Kubrick. Do you know what the chances are of the same disease breaking out in these places, thousands of miles apart, apparently spontaneously, in a matter of days?"

Lou looked at the numbers and shrugged. "Small?"

"With 99% statistical confidence limits, smaller than one in a billion, probably a lot less. This is no natural event."

"I was coming to the same conclusion. So, the question is, if it's not the work of Mother Nature, who is doing this and why?" said Lou, looking to Luciano, who appeared to be even more puzzled.

"*Who?* you ask," said Sergio. "I have a few possible candidates."

Another mouse click and the screen dissolved to what could have been a complex corporate organization chart, with a large blank box at the top. Names and titles, in neat little boxes, were connected with a series of colour coded arrows, some leading to more blanks or question marks. Slide after slide, layer upon layer of data cascaded onto the screen, rendering the final image to an incomprehensible maze.

"I know some of these people," said Lou in astonishment. "Some of them were at the global bioterrorism conference last year. I had to miss that one. Great Uncle Sergio, do you know what happened there?"

"Some *Schifosa* from Germany opened her big mouth and blabbed about the shipment. *Facia bruta!*" said Sergio, with an uncharacteristic red flush of his face.

"What shipment? What's the big-a deal?" said Luciano.

"There was a top secret shipment of one of the most virulent pathogens ever discovered, a vicious type of the pneumonic plague called *Yersinia pestis* strain MF157," said Sergio. "Pneumonic plague can kill you in a day or two. This one is virtually 100% fatal and it only takes a few hours."

"That's some-a virus!"

"Bacteria, Uncle Luciano. You may not care when you're sick, but it makes a big difference to an epidemiologist."

"So, this overly talkative speaker stood up in front of 200 people and started to babble on about the shipment, the routes from Zurich to Atlanta and Winnipeg, the dates, and wouldn't it be awful if some *Al-Jebrah* terrorist got their hands on it. Two days later it was stolen."

"*Puttana!*" said Luciano.

"*Puttana!*" echoed Lou, quickly followed by, "Oops! Sorry."

"So, that's probably the bug that's behind the plagues. The pathophysiology is dead on, no pun intended. So, why can't labs identify it directly?" said Sergio. "Luigi, look at these names again, tell me what you think."

Lou took several minutes to read the charts carefully. "This is so complex, so many relationships to analyze, it would take days. And there are so many unknowns. But let me risk a few generalizations. The largest and richest nations are all represented, executives from most of the world's top multinational corporations, some very old money, and some *nouveau riche*, and extremely powerful families, to say the least. This is a portrait of a global aristocracy. They are so powerful as to be untouchable. Any attempt to attack them directly or arrest any of them would be met with derisive laughter and their allies would back them up immediately. We would be the ones who end up in jail. Who *is* this organization?"

Sergio stared at him. "Don't tell me you've never heard of this group, Luigi."

"I'm not sure. From time to time I hear about some paranoid conspiracy theory with a colourful name. Something like, The Quadrilateral Commission, or The Blunderbuss Group. Wait—most recently somebody said it's supposed to be called the New World Order. From the look of some of those European and Asian families, we should call it the Old World Order."

Sergio laughed out loud, and then gave Lou another smack on the head. "Wonderful, wonderful, that's exactly what they want you to think. Then they can make you run around like a mad dog chasing its tail trying to uncover the secret plan behind machinations behind the plot behind the nefarious scheming behind the conspiracy, and so on forever while the real business goes unnoticed."

"You mean to say that all the rumours that pop up on the internet and in the tabloid press or on trash TV are nothing more than a smokescreen?"

"Precisely! In the past the rumours were generated to implicate the Catholics, or the Freemasons, the Jews, the Knights Templar, Illuminati, and now Islamic conspiracy theories are popular. Sometimes the rumours are even attached to legitimate groups, like some economic think tanks. It has no name, so make one up if you like." Sergio took off his glasses and rubbed his eyes. "Luigi, if you wanted to keep some big plot secret, would you rent some public space or a hotel for big meetings, leak a few tantalizing details to the press?"

"Of course not. So how did you find out who's who? And what are they truly trying to accomplish?"

"Sit back and relax, Luigi, Luciano, this will take a few minutes. People have been fighting for power and dominance for as long as there have been people. It's in our nature. But a couple of centuries ago, it took a sinister turn. After the American and French Revolutions, some of the aristocracy and nobility could see the writing on the wall, and the rise of democracy meant the decline of the privileged classes, and what they would call the inevitable evolution toward rule by mobs and criminal gangs."

"Sure, democracy has its problems, but what do they want to put in its place, a global dictatorship?"

"More like a global oligarchy, rule by a select group from within the conspirators themselves, as it was when only rich, white landowners could vote in America. The conspiracy has been going on for over 200 years, and they kept stalling, mainly due to internal bickering. Ask your friend Brulé just how much the Sherpas usually accomplish in a meeting, and this bunch is no better. Also, their plans were foiled by the increasing power of the ballot, a free press, world wars, cold wars, and so on. Some of them began to have grave doubts about their plan after Hitler, Mao, and other dictators seemed to make democracy look better and better. Finally, in the last few decades, the world started to get richer and richer, at least on paper, without the help of a global oligarchic powerhouse. The ultra rich were doing phenomenally well via the banking system and globalisation without wasting any energy conspiring. A decade or two ago, I began to suspect that there was no more conspiracy to worry about."

"So, what happened to change their plans?"

"Bear with me. I could not sort this out all alone, and there are very few people I can trust with complete confidence, beyond you two and a couple of other members of our extended family. Herb Thicket's death was a terrible loss to us, and I suspect they knew he may have been on to something. I have a few other reliable colleagues in the diplomatic corps, a few academics, and a very few selected contacts in the NSA, CSIS, MI6, and so on. My role in the counter conspiracy, if we can call it that, was to collect and analyze data from the various sources and look for who is doing what, patterns and trends in the data and electronic chatter. Luigi, in a short time this turned from a vague plan to take over the world someday in the future to a specific plan with dates, place names, and marching orders. Our data are incomplete, and some are corrupt, but we pieced it all together as far as possible. A few words keep repeating, and bits of apparently key data have circulated among this conspiratorial network. You want a specific example? Look at this and tell me what you think."

A graph with X and Y axes appeared on the monitor, but no scales. A red line crawled across the bottom and suddenly shot up almost vertically.

Lou looked at it closely and smiled. "This, I recognize. It's a hockey stick graph."

Sergio raised an eyebrow.

"Sorry, it's a Canadian thing. The exponential-like curvature of it appears to fit the shape of the world population growth graph from prehistoric times to the present. It also correlates with the curves for global warming, atmospheric CO_2 levels, rate of species loss, and other environmental issues."

"Bravo, Luigi!" said Sergio. "At least somebody in this family is paying attention." He gave Luciano a playful smack on the head. "I did a regression analysis—call it some voodoo math if you like—and you're right, it fits the best estimates of the human population growth exactly. So, Luigi, why do these aristocratic conspirators care about your *hockey stick* graph? What do you think that's all about?"

Lou paused a moment in thought before replying.

"Bear with me if I ramble on a bit. Sorry. The *Limits to Growth* problem, how and when to put the brakes on unbridled growth in a finite world, is the ghost at the table, the elephant in the room, the thing no one wants to talk about," said Lou. "Everyone worries about the environment, right? So what do we do? We talk, and research all manner of phenomena, all well and good. We come up with all kinds of ways to save the world: recycle, get an electric car, plant some trees. All good ideas but if we accept that human activity is largely responsible for global warming, toxic waste, species loss, and so on, then it should be obvious to almost anyone that the more people there are in the world the more damage will result. But the next step of the syllogism is unthinkable. So, we put on blinders and try to think of something else. Everybody would just love an easy technological fix. 'Please, Mr. Scientist, think of a neat high tech solution so I don't have to think or do anything uncomfortable.' So they gave us solutions like the so called agricultural green revolution in the 1960s, which dramatically increased crop yields. In a perverse sense it just made things worse. Now, instead of three billion people to feed we have eight billion, not to mention who knows what environmental damage from fertilizers, pesticides, and high tech monoculture agriculture. Some estimates suggest we passed the carrying capacity of the earth sometime in the 1980s. We don't want to think about what that means, we just want to keep on living the way we have been living, and not have to give up our precious cars, monster homes, and fresh fruit in January flown in on jet airplanes."

Sergio returned the screen to the hockey stick graph.

Luciano shook his head. "Luigi, how we get here so fast, eh?"

"Good question. We've been great at lowering the death rate with better nutrition, public health, immunization, antibiotics, etc., but generally we've done a lousy job of lowering the birth rate. This is not brain surgery, it's simple math! Biologists get it. Economists do not. Most economists are obsessed with endless growth and pay no heed to the simple fact that we are living on the surface of a finite sphere that isn't getting any bigger."

Luciano interrupted. "But the rich do more damage, *si?*"

"Of course, consumer consumption, water use, CO_2 output, all those are important. But we all do some damage. Everybody eats and creates waste. Even if we all lived like subsistence farmers, there is

73

still a limit to how many people the earth can support in the long run. Some experts say about one or two billion, tops. Some say a few hundred million. If we wanted to turn the earth into a giant feedlot for the maximum possible number of mass produced humans, we could handle a billion more. But putting our fingers in our ears and ignoring the overpopulation issue is like scrubbing the decks on the Titanic while the ship is sinking."

"Luigi, why canna we just all agree we gonna slow down?" said Luciano.

"No disrespect intended, Uncle Luciano, but you said it yourself earlier. We Sicilians don't want to let the Sardinians take over, so we have to make lots of little Sicilians to protect ourselves. China worries about too many Indians, North America is petrified of being overrun by Latin Americans, the Christians are terrified at the thought of being outnumbered by Muslims, and vice-versa, and so on around the world. We evolved in small, competitive tribes as a survival strategy, and we still behave as if we were living on the African savannah. We descended from ancestors who were utterly obsessed with sex and reproduction, and so are most of us today. If there were any humans who were not so fanatical about sex, they went extinct. Lord knows why."

"Then what canna we do?" said Luciano.

"Nothing," said Lou. "The *Limits to Growth* problem, especially population growth, is without an effective solution, and it will be our downfall. I would give anything for a real answer. Some people say 'education is the answer,' which is just another way of dumping the problem onto educators, like we do to scientists, so they don't have to think about it themselves. This would be a much harder sell than teaching trigonometry or tap dancing, and we can't even teach simple stuff like that very well. Even if education and empowering women had some degree of success, the official projections still go up to over nine billion, some say over eleven billion. We were over-using our renewable resources at about four or five billion, some non-renewable resources are starting to run out now, so the global population has to collapse soon. If you think counselling people to have smaller families is easy, just try telling people to stop reproducing, or even slow down, and see what happens. The primitive part of the human brain takes over and they become defensive, or even hostile. It's utterly hopeless if we can't even have a global, rational, discussion about how many people the earth can support. If we cannot solve the population problem, it does not matter what other problems we can solve, the Titanic is still leaking and the game is lost. The biological bottom line is that we humans are animal entities and we behave like any other organism, and will continue to mindlessly reproduce until we completely despoil our environment, run out of arable land and potable water, or get wiped out by a pandemic. It would be nice if that happened while the rest of the living planet has some chance of survival. Reality stinks, doesn't it? Sorry. I am forced to conclude that the world is mad and we're all going to die."

Luciano scratched his beard and said, "Sorry, Sergio, Luigi, I don' understand. First we gotta this big fat cat conspiracy, now we talking environment, and-a too many people. So what's the connection?"

Sergio sat back and gestured to Lou.

"I think I've got it," said Lou. "The conspirators were getting richer and richer, bully for them. But these people are not idiots, most of them anyway, so it must have dawned on them that it could not continue forever. They stopped spinning their wheels sometime in the 1990s, when environmental problems were becoming increasingly and obviously serious. They had to act quickly, and put an end to the destruction of the living world by somehow limiting growth, putting the brakes on the population boom."

Sergio smiled, clicked the mouse, and said, "*Bene*, Luigi, *molto bene*. Now look at a recent modification we discovered, on the last part of the population graph. I enlarged it for you and added scales for time and global population total."

"That shows the population peaking at about eight billion, that's about right, but then it instantly drops down to about 1.2 billion—*whoa!* Right about now!"

"The time is approximate, but sometime this year, for sure."

"But that's impossible! Not even a pandemic could act that fast." Lou stood up and began pacing and rubbed his hands nervously. "It's inconceivable. *Nobody* could pull this off. Not *Al Qaeda, Al-Jebrah*, PLO, the *Mossad*, the Chinese, not even the CIA or the old KGB. There are too many technical and management problems that are insurmountable." Lou began to sweat profusely and wiped his forehead with an old grey handkerchief. He resumed pacing at a faster pace.

Luciano snapped his fingers. "Hey, I bet they gonna use a vaccine, like-a they been trying-a push on everybody for swine flu, bird flu, whatever. That's how they gonna knock us all off by giving us a shot of somethin' plenty bad, like that *pestilence* bug."

"Excellent idea, Uncle Luciano, and inoculating us all with *Yersinia pestis* would be one way to kill billions. But there are other problems. It takes weeks, months or even years to immunize billions of people. The logistics are formidable, not to mention financing. People have had so many false alarms about a killer flu, they have become complacent, and the compliance rates are terrible. And as soon as the disease spreads to, say, a million or more people the game is over and the world completely stops taking their so called immunization shots, and it wouldn't take too long before the real conspirators are exposed. They could even end up killing themselves in the process."

"So how they gonna do it?" said Luciano.

"It just can't be done! There is no practical way of killing billions of people so quickly and still protecting the perpetrators. The whole idea is so disturbing, so awful to contemplate; it's going to take me a while to digest it."

"Luigi, now you know almost as much as me. But there is one word, a key term, maybe a code of some sort, that keeps coming up in the intelligence data we have gathered, and we cannot determine what it has to do with the rest of the plan." Sergio paused and then said, "Do you know what they might mean by a *telomere?*"

Lou grinned nervously, rubbed his hands harder and said, "Of course, it's a basic term in biology, it simply refers to—"

Lou froze, stopped breathing for almost a minute, and as the blood drained from his face he exhaled a primal "Nooooo . . ." and collapsed onto the floor.

Luciano and Sergio helped him into a chair and poured a sip of brandy into his mouth. After a few moments he regained his composure.

"*OK!* I'm OK. Sorry about that. Great Uncle Sergio, I think I've got it, the piece of the puzzle that might just make this conspiracy work," said Lou. He took another sip of brandy. "Suppose you are an environmentalist, albeit an insane, megalomaniac one. You accept that the sheer numbers of people are a primary cause of environmental damage. In order to save the living planet, while there is still time, you decide you need to rub out a few billion people."

"Wow! That's some big-a contract!" said Luciano with a whistle.

"Plus or minus a margin of error of a few hundred million people," added Lou. "The point is the graph doesn't drop to zero, so they don't want to kill everybody, especially not themselves. Behind every suicide bomber is a fat old guy with a grey beard who looks after number one. The only effective way of killing billions of people quickly is by a plague, but how do you protect yourself?"

"Impossible, unless you wanna live in a glass bubble all-a your life," said Luciano.

"But suppose you found a way of engineering a deadly bug with an off switch. Think about what happened to me in the Bahamas, and what happened to some of the people in Stromboli. We got sick and then the pathogens just disappeared. That's where the telomere comes in."

"Hey, Luigi, where am I gonna get myself one of these tell-a-mare things?" said Luciano.

"*Teel*-oh-meer," said Lou. "They're in most of the cells of your body. It's the part of your chromosome that limits the number of times a cell can reproduce."

Sergio spoke up. "Now I'm lost. Slow down and explain."

"It's basic biology, but with a diabolical twist. We are all composed of cells with genetic material inherited from our mothers and fathers. We keep living and growing because our cells can divide and make new cells. The chromosomes copy themselves and the cell splits into two. Grade 9 science, so far, right?"

"*Bene.*"

"So far so good."

"But here's the catch. In the centre of our chromosomes is a part called a centromere. Similarly, on the end of our chromosomes is a little cap, like the aglet on the end of a shoelace, called a telomere. Every time a cell divides, the telomere gets a little shorter. When there is no more telomere left, say after 50 or so divisions, the cell cannot divide, and it breaks up and dies."

Lou took another sip of brandy and wiped the sweat off his forehead. "Aging and death are enormously complicated, of course, but the telomere is a key reason why we don't live forever, but bacteria can. We have them but bacteria don't, so we have to die eventually, but they can just keep on dividing forever like little robots. But, if someone could restructure bacterial DNA, put some telomere-like molecular structure into them, then the bacteria would behave in the same way: they would divide 50 or so many times and stop and die. The longer the telomere-like structure at the end of the chromosomes, the more cell divisions, and the more bacteria in total. By controlling the telomere length, they could predict the maximum number of cell divisions."

Sergio's face went white and he poured himself a double brandy. "Assuming that's what's going on, with a bit of simple statistical mathematics, you could easily calculate how many people would become infected from one cell and how many people would die. Some outbreaks could kill a few people, as it did in Hawaii, while other outbreaks could kill millions, maybe in Europe or China. Then the infectious organism itself dies, breaks up into pieces, and there is no evidence."

Luciano poured himself a cognac and said, "In Stromboli, 40 people died and then she's-a stop, like magic."

"And the best labs cannot identify an organism which has burned itself out before they got to it," said Lou.

Sergio clicked to the slide with the global map. "They are testing their theory and it's all going according to plan. All these outbreaks, isolated islands, small numbers, all part of a carefully controlled scientific experiment to test this horrible thing, this monstrosity. They have turned a natural bug into a deadly weapon with the accuracy of a million rifles."

"More like a million shotguns," said Lou, "Sorry."

Sergio continued. "And because of this part of our own molecular structure, the key to the mystery of our natural death, this evil global network may succeed in their scheme."

"The telomere conspiracy," said Lou.

All three sat in silence for some minutes, trying to grasp the enormity of what lay ahead.

"What a species we humans are: so clever, so cunning, so cutthroat," said Lou, stiffening his courage with another sip of brandy. "But the organization and management needed to pull this off in one quick move must be phenomenal. It would have to be done all at once, before the authorities catch on to who it is. Who is the front man? Who could possibly mastermind such an enterprise?"

Luciano snapped his fingers and said to Sergio, "Tell him about-a the mole."

Sergio said, "Ah, yes. Luigi, we don't know who the mastermind is but there is another player undoubtedly connected to him or her. It is most important that you be aware that one of the Sherpas, Sir William Muggeridge-Pepys, insisted that Dr. Jillian Fleming join your team. I've suspected Sir William is connected to the conspiracy, but, as in so many cases, I have no solid proof. What do you think?"

Lou finished his brandy and said, "That may be the best news I've heard all day. But now, enough talk, time to get into action. Great Uncle Sergio, Uncle Luciano, once again I need some help from my family. Let me explain on the way to picking up Lucia and the twins."

He turned to the elderly family patriarch and said, "Great Uncle Sergio, I can't thank you enough for all your help. We few may be the only hope of preventing the brutal murder of seven billion people."

Sergio looked at the graph and said, "The actual figure is only 6.8 billion."

"Thank heavens," said Lou. "I was afraid we might be dealing with extremists."

CHAPTER 6

Countdown to Earth Day

The Global Headquarters of the Mendel Foundation for Ecological Research and Education was located in an older part of the business district of Paris, some distance from the more modern *La Défense*. The foundation's flagship office, a neo-classical building which dated from the early 1800s, was previously owned by a private investment bank, *La Banque des Frères Bulles*. To help present an image of strength, solidity, and stability, the façade was dominated by four Corinthian columns, carved from granite imported from the Canadian Shield, and said to be stronger than Samson. *Les Frères Bulles'* illusion of stability had burst in the last recession.

As the foundation underwent exponential growth over the last few years, dominating the environmental charity business, auxiliary offices gradually took over the nearby premises of several international charitable and non-governmental organizations. Perhaps an accident of growth, or perhaps an instance of public relations, the most dramatic parts of the foundation's activities occurred in the large, old bank foyer. Teens and young adults of all races, all wearing the now familiar *Eco Angels* t-shirts, tapped on computers, shouted into telephones, and held impromptu meetings with the frenzy of a political campaign office just before election day.

Sheila was patiently explaining to a fellow Aussie caller, "It's easy to join, mate! All expenses are paid by the Mendel Foundation. Can I sign you up?" On a nearby shared desk Iqbal was reassuring his caller in Arabic, "You can go anywhere on Earth, Vietnam, Denmark, we need team leaders everywhere!" while his partner Ndugu spoke in a West African French dialect, "How would you like to go to Canada! . . . Sorry, sorry, then how about America? Yes, of course!" If there were any slackers in this largely volunteer staff, they were not in this room at this time.

Banners hung from the ceiling and posters plastered the walls, with glossy bright coloured messages like:

> *Join the Eco Angels and Earn School Credits!*
> *Show Mother Earth We Care!*
> *Yes! WE CAN Save the Earth!*, and
> *Earth Day is Everybody's Birthday!*

Sheila's t-shirt was emblazoned with the message that gave her a reason to live: *NO MATTER WHO YOU ARE, NO MATTER WHERE YOU COME FROM, NO MATTER WHAT YOU HAVE DONE, KARL LOVES YOU.*

Overshadowing all displays was the Big Board, a wall-sized LED screen flashing red, green, yellow and blue colour-codes as key statistics were automatically updated. The data at the top of the board read:

WORLD POPULATION:
7,998,086,758
COUNTDOWN TO EARTH DAY, NOON GMT:
209 hours 29 min. 57 sec.
PLEDGED PARTICIPANTS ~ GLOBAL TOTAL:
6,641,682,037

Lower displays showed Eco Angels Team Captains by country, crossed referenced with numbers of municipalities, reserves, senior centres, hospitals, schools, prisons, and churches, mosques, synagogues and temples. On several plasma monitors were promotional videos showing Eco Angels planting trees with natives, digging wells, cleaning up garbage, feeding the homeless, singing as they work, and visiting and hugging seniors, prisoners, and children in hospitals.

And everywhere, on walls, banners, desks, the plasma monitors, and above all, in people's hearts, was the image of Karl Mendel, the charismatic leader who dedicated his life to do anything, everything, he possibly could, to save the planet we all love.

"HHHEEEYYY! Everyone!" shouted an amazingly animated Ganesh as he ran out of a back room. "Heads up! Heads up! It's KARL!!!"

Ganesh gestured for two Eco Angels in the back room to join him, and wrapped his arms around the svelte blonde Kimberly, who had her t-shirt tied high and tight below her augmented DD teenaged breasts. And then there was Pong. Pong rarely spoke, and the unisex haircut, underweight frame and horn-rimmed glasses gave no clue to his or her sex.

The room burst into cheers, then a chant. "Karl! Karl! Karl! *Yaaayyy* KARL!!"

Karl walked into the room like the rock star of all rock stars he truly was, hands held high and then shaking the many outstretched palms. He raised his hands again and the room fell into reverential silence, until Sheila began sobbing and shouted, "I love you Karl! The whole world loves you!" Iqbal and Ndugu rushed to her comfort, forming a group hug *à trois*.

"Is everyone ready to share the *love* on Earth Day?" shouted Karl with arms outstretched high, first two fingers of each hand pointing in a Nixonian double *V for Victory* sign. The room erupted again in cheers as Karl gave his most modest look and his eyes welled up with tears.

"And tonight," he began, voice cracking with apparent emotion, "tonight on ECO TV, the whole world is going to fall in love with our Eco Angels! Let's hear it for our TV stars: Kimberly, Ganesh and Pong!"

As the room burst into one large climactic cheer, Karl hugged Ganesh and Pong, while Kimberly hugged Karl about the waist and kissed his shirt buttons, slowly working her way south. There was not a dry eye in the room, except for Pong, whose expression suggested that he or she would truly rather be somewhere else, or perhaps that the saviour of the planet had just silently passed some deadly greenhouse gas.

Mr. Loh navigated the stretch mini through the dense traffic as Mr. Lee snapped his cell phone shut.

"Mr. Yang and Mr. Yen are dead," said Mr. Lee, "perhaps because they failed to blend in with the local culture."

"Their clothing may have been too conspicuous," said Mr. Lei from the back seat.

"I think perhaps the style of walking is less common than we had assumed. I see very few people doing the *pimp roll*. Could it have been a passing fad?" chirped in Mr. Lie.

"Focus on the targets," said Mr. Lee, "the gargantuan pugilist and the blonde, no one else."

"A little music to improve the harmony of our operation," said Mr. Lee slipping a CD into the car's stereo.

As the stretch mini approached Lou's office building, the sinister team burst into a barbershop quartet rendition of *All day, all night, I will wait for you.*

Woody tried to project an air of confidence as he took the host's chair. In the Paris ECO TV Studio, a talk show style arrangement of furniture occupied the small stage. Technicians and camera operators attended to their equipment as the last of the audience filled the remaining seats. Finally, the floor director looked at Woody and began a finger countdown from five.

Woody began to speak but was drowned out by the offstage announcer's booming, "It's the Gaia Show! Here's tonight's special guest host, Windrow Logman!"

The applause sign flashed and the 200 strong studio audience burst into a roaring welcome. Woody glanced to his left to see Karl standing in the darkened wings area offstage. From that distance, Woody could not be sure, but it looked like Karl was pulling a hair from his nose with a pair of tweezers. The applause began to die down and Woody faced the camera with the flashing red light.

"Good evening everyone, I'm Woody Logan. It's a great pleasure and indeed an honour to welcome our very special guest, an eminent biologist, environmental champion, and a truly positive role model for young people all around the world. Please give a warm welcome to *Doctor* Karl Mendel!!"

The applause signs flashed furiously as Karl strode onto the stage, beaming with teary eyes. Woody rose to offer a handshake, which Karl morphed into an extended hug.

"Karl, there is so much we could talk about: your books, your foundation, your environmental work with the Eco Angels. You are just so active in so many ways, and I must say, you are are so loved, deeply loved, by all of humanity worldwide."

Tears flowed down Karl's cheeks in parallel tracks, as he faced the camera, covering his mouth with the back of one hand and gesturing an inability to speak with the other.

"How can anyone not love a man who is not afraid to let his truest, deepest feelings show to the world? Don't we just love this guy, folks?"

More applause, sobbing, and feminine cries of "Oh, God, YES we love you Karl!"

Karl regained his composure, wiping his face with a silk handkerchief. "No, please, everyone, you are too kind. I'm just one small person trying to do my little part to help save the planet we all love." Subdued applause, and a few *Aaaahhh*'s.

"We could talk all night long and love every minute of it, but you have a special announcement tonight, don't you? And some special guests?"

"Yes! The real stars of Earth Day—three of our Eco Angels!"

More applause erupted as the three stars, wearing designer Eco Angels track suits, walked cautiously onto the stage. Ganesh and Kimberly had dilated pupils and an other-worldly look about them. Pong made eye contact with no one.

"There they are, the finest young people of their generation. Would you like to start, Karl, or—"

Karl could barely contain himself. "The Angels! The Eco Angels!!"

Kimberly was snuggled up to Karl's shoulder, eyes closed in rapture, Pong stared at the floor with elbows on his or her knees and hands over his or her ears. Ganesh seemed to be in a state of rapture, mouth agape, looking at all the pretty studio lights.

Woody leaned forward with a toothy smile. "Now here's a handsome young man in what I believe is called a track suit, all green and brown earth tones with aqua highlights. I am told it was designed by the famous Icelandic fashion house, *Ship of Fools*. Would you like to tell us about it, Ganesh?"

Ganesh took a deep breath and appeared to address an invisible entity about eight feet above centre stage. "Oh, man, these are so cool! It's all earthy and other righteous stuff like that, and we got them made, Karl got them made, sorry Karl, from workers' communes or kibbutzes, or whatever, track suit factories in North Korea. Wow! North Korea, so like how cool is that! So, the workers, they own all the shares and profits and assets and stuff, because we, I mean Karl, had this really great idea that we should help everybody share all the Earth Day stuff and stuff like that. Not like the stinking filthy capitalist pig corporations that steal all their money from the workers' pockets and off their backs, and stuff, and they're all corrupt and filthy pigs and hate all the real people and the filthy pigs should go to jail or burn in hell or something like that. Yea, Karl! Go, Karl, go! Or whatever."

Woody's mouth was slightly ajar, and he stared at Ganesh as he tried to think of what came next. "Hmmm. North Korea, great idea. Karl, tell us some more."

"Thank you, Woody. Don't you just love our Eco Angels, everyone?"

The applause sign brought only scattered applause, and a few murmurs of *what did that kid say?*

Karl looked like he was on the verge of crying again. "This day, this very special day, . . . I'm sorry, I so overwhelmed by all the love in this room. In this world."

Karl reached for his handkerchief, blew his nose, and pulled out a few more nose hairs.

Woody filled the time with, "We're all eager to hear about the special Earth Day you've got planned for us. Tell us all about it, Karl."

"That's right Woody. We are going to celebrate, people! Celebrate our Mother Earth! And these angels, these beautiful angels all over the world, will join together, Woody, join together in a gigantic *GLOBAL GROUP HUG AROUND THE WORLD!!!* Angels everywhere will be reaching out to the poor, the homeless, the elderly, disrespected minorities, prisoners everywhere, hospitals, refugee camps, native reservations, everyone! Woody, let's show the folks at home and in our audience what we're talking about."

"Of course. The studio audience can see the video on our monitors," said Woody.

"Poor old Mother Earth has been having a rough ride from humanity of late, so we asked ourselves, 'Where do we start the healing?' We start by healing ourselves. By showing every last person on earth that they are truly loved. Here, for example, is Ismael, a child soldier at the tender age of eight, somewhere in East Africa. Can you see the pain behind that surly expression, the cigarette and machine gun in the hands of an innocent youngster?"

They audience moaned a unanimous *Aaaaaaah*!

"Here are Masha and Dinka, a lesbian couple—Woody, do we say lesbian or is it gay couple?"

"The latest I heard this week was *women of queerness.*"

"Ah, the wonderful euphemism treadmill," said Karl. "This once happy couple, and with their combined family of 13 children, sired by irresponsible fathers, pimps and rapists, lost their way in the aftermath of the economic chaos of recent years, clearly victims of lesbo-phobe prejudice and not at all their fault. So sad, their children ripped from their mothers' bosoms and shoved into despicable orphanages, now poor Dinka and poor Masha lead loveless lives in the wretched Russian prison system, where corruption, violence and incurable disease are running amok."

Oooooooh!

"Juan and Maria, and their 11 beautiful children, were forced from their homes in Brazil, and are now forced to eke out a living by clear-cutting forests and subsistence farming somewhere in the Amazon."

Now several audience members were audibly sniffling and sobbing.

"Even the wealthiest country in the world, the U.S. of A., suffers from a lack of love. Little LeRoy was deprived of an education by a heartless school system dominated by white rascist administrators, and he was pressured into a life of crime by the local drug lord, while his little sister, Sin-dour-ella, barely a teenager, had to become a prostitute to provide for her three fatherless children."

Karl wiped the tears from his face, and said, "I'm sorry. Every time I see these people I am completely overcome with emotion. But I must show you Isaac Beaver-Tail, his wife Penny Two-Chins and their nine children, disenfranchised from their traditional way of life, and forced to live on a government funded native reserve where the only recreational activity is sniffing gasoline. And here are a few of the thousands of seniors suffering from dementia, abandoned and held prisoner in mental institutions, barely conscious, force-fed and just waiting for a merciful liberation which may never come. Finally, some of the thousands of illegal immigrant children from Eastern Europe forced to survive on the streets of cities like Madrid and Paris by begging and stealing."

Now Woody was crying, Ganesh was still staring at the invisible entity, and Kimberly was stroking Karl's thigh. Pong had not moved.

"Who among you can possibly say no to the needy of the world?" said Karl, his lower lip trembling. "Let's show every human being on earth that they are loved. Join us, please join us, for our *global group hug* on *Earth Day*. Start by hugging the Eco Angel nearest you, in his or her new track suit, and carry the love to everyone you see. Can you picture that? All around the world, all loving each other at the same time! Millions! Billions sharing the love! Oh, God, God, I am overcome! I—I—I love you all so much!"

Karl collapsed onto Kimberly's bosom, as Woody rubbed him gently on the shoulder.

"Truly, sincerely, Karl you are the most passionate and loving man on this planet. Now a word from our sponsor."

Woody gathered up his guests for a group hug as the Gaia Show's theme music began.

Ganesh whispered to Woody, "Capitalist stooge."

✸

"So now what we suppose to be do-ink, Jill? We have no more leads, our boss gone, and why big rush to go back to office?" Tanya's irritation bounced off the concrete walls of the underground parking garage of Lou's office building. Joe left the Hummer in a shadowed corner and caught up with Tanya and Jill. Only a few other cars remained in the garage, most conspicuously a stretch mini near the elevator.

"Listen, we are all over tired and thoroughly stressed, trust me. We need a new environment, some food and a chance to relax," said Jill. "I might try my contact at the PMO on the secure line."

"Is very spiffy idea, just smashing and jolly good. Maybe we forget all about missing Lou and enjoy selves, have party, *da*?"

"Oh, fiddlesticks! Sorry, mates, I've forgotten my bag. Carry on, I'll catch up." Jill trotted back to the Hummer, and around to the far side.

Four Asian men in Hip Hop attire, carrying identical automatic pistols, emerged in unison from the stretch mini, humming an old Bing Crosby tune.

Joe dropped his packages and shouted to Tanya, "Get down!" Before he could draw his pistol, a black delivery van screeched into the garage with its horn honking, and expertly spun though a 90° turn, stopping between Joe, Tanya and the assassins. The van erupted in gunfire, slicing the Hip Hop boys down before they had landed a shot remotely near their original targets. A heap of four bling laden bodies now lay on the concrete floor, gushing blood, which quietly formed a large, crimson, elliptical pool, with one small rivulet reaching a floor drain near the van.

"Joe, it's me. Don't shoot, please."

"Lou? You OK?" Joe holstered his pistol and helped Tanya to her feet. They rushed to the far side of the van to look at the carnage.

"Just fine, thank you." Lou gestured for the other occupants of the van to come out. Jill rushed back from the Hummer to join them, her face a picture of utter astonishment.

"We have a lot of catching up to do, but it only seems right to start with some introductions. Tanya, Joe, Jill. I'd like you to meet my family. This is my Uncle Luciano, my late father's older brother, my cousins Enrico and Mario, and yes, they are twins. And last but by no means least, our expert driver, my cousin Lucia from Goose Bay."

"Goose Bay?" queried Jill.

Luciano responded, "Lucia di Labrador."

The team of now eight people came together as a group, stepping carefully around the four bodies, exchanging greetings, handshakes, and hugs, with impeccable manners, gingerly sidestepping the large pool of blood.

Hello. Pleased to meet you. My pleasure. How nice to meet you. Splendid. Buon Giorno! Charmed, I'm sure. Enchanted. Anyone hungry? Oops! Watch your step. Mind the messy pool of blood. May I offer you a tissue?

As the pleasantries continued, Lou pulled Joe aside, toward the Hummer, and whispered in his ear.

"Joe, I need you to do a job for me, something very special."

Karl left the ECO TV studio by a rear entrance, dabbing his nose with a handkerchief, as he saw his limousine approaching from a block away.

"Hello? *Bonsoir?* Yes, my one and only salacious singularity of seduction. Great! It went perfectly. But I think I may have a nosebleed—I pulled out too many nose hairs when I was trying to get the tears rolling on cue."

Mei was lounging in her bright red silk pyjamas and Persian slippers, buffing her fingernails with a baby Panda-skin chamois, sitting by the speakerphone in Karl's library. "Sorry to call you on your cell phone, Karl, but this can't wait."

"Uh-oh, cell phones are not at all secure. Choose your words carefully, love pumpkin of my dreams."

"Your friend the mole has some good news: the Hip Hop duo said nothing and are now *pimp rolling* in heaven. Now the bad news: guess who popped up again?"

"A dismal spirit, a lu-gu-brious ghost, my potato?"

"Potato? You just called me a potato? Is that what you genuinely think of me? ME?" Mei's brow furrowed and her eyes narrowed to the thickness of a razor blade.

"Sweet potato! Sweetest of the sweetest sweet potatoes! I only have eyes for you, O root vegetable of all my desire, tingling tuberous target of my throbbing tumescence!" Karl mopped a few beads of sweat from his forehead.

"That's better. Yes, him. Now the really bad news. He's back and with reinforcements. Big time. Says they are 'family.'"

"How much does he know, O bountiful goddess of the harvest moon?"

"She's not sure yet. Big boxing boy and the blond bean counter got grumpy after the Smart Car boys grew wings. The spook hasn't spoke. And it gets worse. Four more harps in heaven. A quaternion on high."

"I absolutely hate cell phones at times like this. Try that last point again, my randy archangel of divine lust."

"The barbershop quartet. *La-la-la-la!* Quartered. Gone to their harmonious reward. Now in the heavenly choir, singing *A Closer Pimp Roll With Thee*." Mei gave herself a yummy hug for that one.

"This is bad, very, very bad. The mole needs to bolt before they put the screws to her. We can't afford to lose her."

"So you care more about *her* than *me*? **ME?!?**"

"Never give her a second thought, my twinkle in the evening star. But she does have a certain strategic value, my precious, pulsating, pearl of pulchritude. Have Mr. 'Mucky-Pup' recall her. Gotta go." The limousine stopped beside Karl, and DeWang opened the rear door for him.

"OK, but wait, wait! Karl? Do you love me? Say it, Karl. 'But screw your courage to the sticking place' and spit it out, big boy. Tell me you love me. I just have to hear you say the L-word."

"L-later."

Mei punched the *off* button of the speakerphone with a sharp jab.

"How do you like that. He never tells me he loves me. *Men! Oh!*"

Meanwhile, on the other side of the ECO TV studio, Woody was beaming with fantasies of a new career as a talk show host. The studio doorman handed him an envelope which Woody tore open and read the note, hand written on fine linen stationery.

"Oh gosh, it's from Karl. ' . . . loved meeting you so much . . . . exclusive interview at my château! . . . Mr. Park will take care of you.' WOW! I can't believe this is happening."

An Asian man in Hip Hop attire *pimp-rolled* up to Woody. "Mr. Logan? My name is Park. I believe you're expecting me."

"Yes! Mr. Park. You work for Dr. Mendel?"

"Indeed. Please accept his apologies for not greeting you personally. He had an urgent matter to take care of. I would be honoured if you would allow me to escort you to his château, a considerably long drive but I hope we can make it a pleasant one for you. Please walk this way."

Mr. Park *pimp-rolled* Woody around a short block and into a nearby alley. Strange, thought Woody, that so many street lights needed replacing.

A small tourist bus was parked in the shadows. As Woody paused to read the sign on the bus—*North Korea People's Free Will Glee Club*—seven more Hip Hop boys emerged from the shadows. Mr. Park took out his pitch pipe, blew an F-sharp, and his colleagues began to hum *Jerusalem* as they surrounded Woody.

Mr. Park opened the bus door, gave a small bow toward Woody, and said, "Would you be kind enough to join us, Mr. Logan?"

Woody suffered another brief moment of dissociation, picturing himself as an emaciated POW in a North Korean prison camp, trying to catch a rat for dinner. *Think of something fast.*

"OK, sure. Oh, heck! I forgot to phone my Mom after the show. Darn it. She gets awfully mad if I don't call her. Why don't I just rent a car and, uh, and—"

"The intended mood of my sentence was imperative, not interrogative, Mr. Logan."

The gang of eight drew the human net closer. Woody acquiesced and entered the bus with a nervous, high pitched laugh. The others followed, sandwiching their guest in tightly. Mr. Park took the driver's seat, and blew a long note with his pitch pipe.

"Mr. Logan, please join in," he said as the bus pulled out of the alley.

Woody's crackling counter tenor tried to keep up with the Glee Club's polished performance.

> "*And did those feet in ancient time,*
> *Walk upon England's mountains green?*
> *And was the holy Lamb of God,*
> *On England's pleasant pastures seen?*"

Karl rubbed his hands with glee in the rear of his limousine, and turned on the radio. Neville Lear's polished tones oozed from the speakers.

". . . who, of course, is well known to all of our listeners. Welcome to *Public Perceptions* on ECO FM radio, your highness."

"Your Royal Highness, if you bolly-wolly well please, you uppity twit." Monty's well known voice sent a chill down Karl's spine.

"Oh, Lord, NO!! Please, please no! He's going to spill the beans on everything!" In his panic, Karl rolled down his side window and shouted to his chauffeur, "Step on it, DeWang, we've got a problem."

Karl passed the tour bus, and heard nine harmonious voices singing.

> *". . . Bring me my chariot of fire!*
> *I will not cease from Mental Fight,*
> *Nor shall my Sword sleep in my hand,*
> *Till we have built Jerusalem, ..."*

Neville sat across a small table from Monty, an unobtrusive overhead microphone for each. Three technicians monitored the program from within a glass booth.

"My abject apologies, Your Royal Highness."

"You must learn to show proper respect for your betters."

"If you would be so kind, your Eminence, would you care to share with our listeners your vision of the future and hopes for humanity?"

"I can tell you what my vision is in one word—crowded! The whole wretched planet is hugger-mugger with useless yobbos."

"Your Magnificence sees the population issue, then, as being of paramount importance?"

"If there were such a thing as reincarnation, I would return as a deadly virus and decrease the surplus population."

"Then the sheer numbers of people—"

"It's not just the numbers, you arty-farty, boot-licking radio wallah. As my late wife Ethne was fond of saying, bless her and her frugal family, we need to concentrate on quality, not quantity. The entire human gene pool is going down a disgusting drain called dysgenics. It's all the frogs and wogs, bog trotters, dagos, micks and spics, hunkies and Russkies, kikes and camel jockeys, eggplants and redskins, squareheads and pissant towelheads. And all the sodomites and catamites, poncey sausage jockeys, arse bandits, turd burglars and fudge packers, fur burger-licking carpet munchers, gormless imbeciles, morons, geeks, cretins and retards, ne'er do well derelicts and sycophantic panhandlers. Into the marble orchard with the works of them. Put them all six feet under!"

Neville signalled to the technicians to cut off Monty's microphone, and whispered directly into his own mike as Monty continued babbling in the background.

"And there it is, indeed, a vision of the future and what hope remains for us therein, most eloquently and uniquely expressed, perhaps with some singular metaphorical phrasing, by His Royal Highness. We are looking forward to his Grace's keynote speech at the *Global Conference on the Future*."

Monty was oblivious to Neville's manoeuvre. "The smeg head poofters and woolly woofters, pea brains, schizos, rug rats, stroppy old trouts, bungling bureaucrats, workhouse whangers, wacky crack heads, Kaffirs, whirling dervishes, fuzzy-wuzzies, nogoodniks and greasers, vegetables, blinks and freaks and fruitcakes, bug house ding-a-lings, ning nongs and ping pongs, wet-backs, wimps, gimps and crips, loony toonies, thugs and slugs. And worst of all, the sub-human colonials who are so preposterous as to believe we are all equal! Off with all their heads! Wankers! Dingleberries and will-nots!

The theme music chimed in and the *OFF THE AIR* sign flashed on.

Neville leaned over to Monty and quietly asked, "Is there anyone on earth you *do* like?"

In a quiet suburban neighbourhood, Joe's Hummer pulled up to the rear of a stately funeral home, a Victorian era house with an illuminated stained-glass window reading *Burke's Mortuary and Crematorium*. The receiving doors opened wide and the octogenarian Harry Burke pushed out a large dolly.

"Joe, old friend, it's been ages. Lou said you have a couple of customers for me."

"They keep multiplyin' like flies, Harry." He opened the rear door of the Hummer and two body bags tumbled out. "Now we got six customers for you. Hey, Harry, check out these new body bags. All natural fibre, hemp mostly, they got no toxic chemicals, and all made with good pay for the workers in some co-op in Argentina. Yah know, Harry, it's all the little things like this that makes you feel like the world is moving in the right direction some days. Nice, eh?"

"Excellent, Joe, a vast improvement over the old, clear plastic ones. There are few things I like more, in my old age, than a well-made body bag. Just stack them right here, please, Joe."

"At least these guys don't weigh much. Remember two years ago? Samoans! They were the worst. And they cursed like crazy, and used all the baddest swear words." Joe picked up the first bag with one hand and tossed it onto the dolly. "The Samoans had to be at least three or four hundred pounds each, all 12 of them. Give me these skinny little Hip Hop Rappin' weirdos any day. I could get a dozen of these guys these in the back of the Hummer, easy. Maybe eighteen if we did a tight head to toe stack." Joe piled the rest of the body bags containing the mortal remains of the late Hip Hop boys onto the dolly, and pulled them over to the crematorium furnace. "There's another box for you in the passenger seat. It's got all the guns and bling and stuff."

Harry flipped a wall switch and with a *whoosh!* the furnace flames popped on. "Big or small, well or ill, these late gentlemen will soon all be ashes for landfill," he said. Harry lifted a sheet from a nearby gurney. "Have a look at this, Joe, while the hell fires are warming up."

Joe did a double take at the sight of a large, naked, male corpse. "Whoa! Is this the guy I'm supposed to meet?"

"No, this is the late Mr. Hoskins, who is scheduled for cremation tonight. Have a close look at him, Joe. Mr. Hoskins is approximately your size, and with a little hair dye and liposuction, he would be an excellent match. I do think he looks like you, doesn't he, Joe?" Harry kneaded his arthritic hands and smiled at his guest's discomfort. "Oh, my, you are perturbed at the sight of your doppelganger in a mortuary, aren't you? Follow me, please. The man you are looking for is very much alive. Walk this way."

Harry shuffled in tiny arthritic steps, leading Joe from the crematorium, past embalming tables with several bodies in various stages of preparation, to the cosmetics and dressing area. He knocked three times on a wooden door, and said, "Your guest has arrived, sir."

The door opened and Sergio Spenalzo beckoned Joe to enter. Two young bodyguards in silk suits and slicked back hair, Bruno and Rocco, gave Joe cautious smiles.

"Hello, Joe. My name is Sergio. You may call me Serge, if you like."

"A pleasure, sir. I'm not sure what we're supposed to be doing."

"We were just looking at some of Mr. Burke's suits," said Sergio, pulling a large, shiny, brown three piece suit from a long rack. I think this will do nicely."

"Sorry, I don't understand what's going on. Lou didn't tell me much."

Sergio smiled. "Joe, I hear you like to do magic tricks."

Antonio's official story was that he kept the back room of his bar and restaurant for special occasions such as small wedding receptions and private parties. Most of the time it was held in reserve for Don Luciano Gubriace.

Antonio served his special guests personally, and tonight nothing was too good for Don Luciano's party. Lucia, Mario and Enrico shared massive platters of *pasta* and *risotto*, bowls of *insalata verde*, *pesce, carne di manzo, prosciutto*, and, for ethnic variety, several baskets of crispy, Cajun-style deep-fried chicken.

"*Mangia, mangia*, you gonna need your strength," said Luciano. He gestured to Tanya, who sat alone at the opposite end, nibbling on a bread stick and tapping on her computer. "Poor little Russia' girl, you gonna fade away to nuttin', *too-var-itch*, eat, eat!" He gestured toward Jill, who was engaged in an animated discussion on the pay phone, but could not entice her to come to the table.

Magda strolled around playing *Funiculi funicula* on her violin, with occasional lusty glances in Luciano's direction.

Lou stood a few feet from a large screen TV, remote control firmly attached to his hand, watching the broadcast of Woody's interview with Karl and the Eco Angels. Jill hung up the pay phone, dropped her purse on her chair, rushed over to Lou, and tapped him on the shoulder.

"You blokes just can't stop watching that box, can you? Where's Joe tonight?" she said with an impish smile.

"Joe had to drop off our would-be assassins to the crematorium. He should be along anytime soon."

On the screen, Kimberly was snuggling up to Karl. Lou shook his head.

"Look at that girl! She's in love with a guy old enough to be her father. And the women in the audience, they can't get enough of him. Jill, you're a psychiatrist. Can you tell me why women find this Mendel guy so irresistible? I don't get it," said Lou with a shrug.

"No accounting for taste, I suppose. The girl's probably damaged goods looking for the real father she never had. A week or so from now she'll flip and see him as the monster daddy from hell. Personally, I think Mendel's an overrated, overblown, egomaniacal attention seeker, and he'll be old news next month. And just look at that sycophantic little catamite TV boy he keeps at his side, like a trained monkey."

Jill looked about the room and dropped her voice to an excited whisper. "Lou, listen, this is great news. I just spoke to my contact at the PMO. He's utterly aghast at the attempts on our lives."

"News? What's he got?" Lou clicked off the TV, Tanya passed some breadsticks to Luciano, and Mario and Enrico swatted each other, got up and started to play Sumo, blocking Jill's view of her purse.

"Get this!" Jill stood on her tiptoes, trying to come up to Lou's level. "He says they picked up a likely suspect with an automated body language scan at Gatwick, and tentatively connected him to an Iranian or Pakistani terrorist cell. It seems he chartered a special flight to Kubrick Island from the U.K. and left just before we got there, flew straight back to Gatwick. When they caught him he was carrying some biological material in a high tech case marked *Live Transplant Organs*."

Lucia slipped something into Jill's purse and nodded to her uncle. Luciano stepped between Enrico and Mario and smacked them each on the head. "Hey, break it up, you gorillas, before somebody gonna get hurt. Finish you din-dins."

Lou appeared to be momentarily distracted by Luciano's boys, then turned his attention back to Jill. "This is fantastic! Was there anything viable left? Have they analyzed the material?"

"There was something suspicious in the case, but the techno-weenies are still performing the analysis. They've been making him perspire buckets, but he's a pretty tough nut, and hasn't divulged anything significant so far. But listen, Lou, here's the best part: this chap wants to make a deal!"

"Sure, he wants to save his own skin. What's the offer?"

"He's engaged a solicitor, but it appears to be the usual demands—immunity from prosecution, a few million quid, and witness protection program in some nondescript, boring backwater where he can safely spend the rest of his life in obscurity, someplace like Tonga, Togo, Tortuga, or—"

"Toronto?" said Lou.

"Yes, perfect," said Jill. "In return we get all the details, names, dates, locations, and some Mr. Big who's masterminded the whole thing. The whole shebang!" Jill gave Lou a double arm squeeze and an excited smile.

"Everything we want on a silver platter," said Lou, adding a low whistle.

"But the PMO wants me in London ASAP to be in on the interrogation and debriefing. No drugs, nothing risky. I'm so excited! I want to use a brilliant new protocol developed in Australia. The Aussies call it *The Melbourne Method*. They want me to read him, make sure he's giving us everything."

"It sounds too good to be true, but we can't miss this. Go for it, Jill, and update us as soon as you can."

"I can catch a diplomatic flight within the hour." She gave Lou a kiss on the cheek, grabbed her bag and headed for the door.

"Ta-ta for now, everyone, must fly!"

As soon as Jill was out the door, Lou put his finger to his lips and the room fell silent. After a few seconds, he turned to Tanya. "Did you get all of that?"

"Fee, fie, foe, fum, Lou, I smell big stinkin' English crock of lies." Tanya cracked her knuckles and read from her laptop screen. "No special charters in Kubrick for at least six days before we get there. Was first thing I check. And no courier picked up conveniently by MI5, MI6, Scotland Yard or Sheer-luck Holmes. No biological material in convenient case."

"Positive, no mistakes?" said Lou.

"Absolutely. Jill story complete fabrication, makes everything as easy as cake—like murder mystery with too neat ending."

"Now we wait," said Lou, "and listen."

The only sound in the room was the ticking of Antonio's grandfather clock.

Jill rushed out of Antonio's with her purse and medical bag tucked under one arm, and waved in vain for a taxi with the other. The Hummer pulled around the corner, parked on the far side of the street, and Joe stepped out, wearing a shiny brown suit and two tone brown and cream shoes.

Jill smiled and waved at him, and said under her breath, "No more fashion sense than a dromedary camel, I swear."

Joe waved back, and got as far as saying "Hiya, Ji—" when all hell broke loose.

A dark red delivery truck with no license plates screeched around the corner, stopping in front of Joe. Shouts of *Cornuto! Cornuto!* were almost drowned out by the sound of automatic gunfire. As the truck pulled away, a large explosion engulfed the Hummer in flames, so powerful that Jill could feel the shock wave and the heat from across the street. It took a moment for her to regain her composure, and then she could see a large man lying on the pavement, so engulfed in flames that only parts of his shiny brown suit and two tone shoes were visible.

Lou rushed out of the restaurant first, followed by his family and Tanya. Enrico and Mario had their pistols drawn.

"Jill, are you OK? What happened?"

Jill was now trembling, and could barely get her words out. "It's Joe, I just saw him and waved and then they came, and, and it was too fast, it was awful, Lou I don't—"

"OK, it's OK now," said Lou.

Luciano put his arm around Jill. "I'm-a thinkin' it was-a Sardinians. They do the contract killings. Maybe they come after the rest of us, now. Enrico, get the van, Mario, you cover him. Sardinians, they're the worst."

"Jill, you've got to get out of here. It's too dangerous to stay with us. Go do your job—you can only get killed if you stay. Go!" Lou watched her bolt around the corner.

Tanya whispered, "Now what, Lou?"

"Now we go fishing, with our beautiful, British bait.'

Far down the road, a short conversation occurred in the red delivery truck.

"Hey, that word you shouted, *Cornuto*, that's not a bad word, is it? Is it a curse word?"

"Oh, no, it means we *like* you, *we really like you!*"

CHAPTER 7

The L-word

Jill changed taxis twice, and had the last cab drop her near a phone booth at a small city park. The usual assortment of punks and beggars were kept in line by frequent police patrols. An inebriated busker, whose handlebar moustache made him look like a character out of a comic opera, was playing *La Vie en Rose* on his accordion. Jill looked about nervously as she placed a call.

From the back of his limousine on an express highway toward his château, Karl was contemplating his next move when his cell phone rang with an *applause* ring tone.

"Hello, *bonsoir*?"

"I know you don't like me to call you on your cell, especially at this hour, but this can't wait," said Jill.

"Ah, the perils of unsecured calls," said Karl, admiring his manicure, "choose your words carefully, love demon of my dreams."

"Good news: I've managed to jump ship and I can be flapping my wings to your lair in a tick."

"Change of plans, O succubus of my slumbers. Dumbo of the Major Leagues has flapped his ears in your direction. He's about to open his trunk, trumpet to the world, and spill the big biological beans. *Comprenez-vous*?"

"I utterly abhor cell phones. *Parli Inglese, Signore? Mein Herr?*"

"OK. *You-know-who,* Mr. Filthy Lucre, is in your town. About to tell all to the world. Ev-er-y-thing? Remember the conference, my grand angel of the Inquisition?"

"Now, I get it. Good heavens, he's such an asinine bigot, will anyone listen to him or even understand a word he says?"

"We can't risk it at this stage, beautiful bludgeon of my bones. You can't let him make his big speech. Stop the twit, somehow. Tie him up if you have to."

"What a delicious image," said Jill with a lick of her canine teeth. "Perhaps I shall fashion a Gordion Knot out of barbed wire."

"You're as sweet as a razor, my stropable Jill-ette. Sorry, no rough stuff with Mister Money-bags. Keep him healthy, very happy, and eager to sign more big, beautiful cheques."

"Got it, big guy. I'll treat him like the royalty he thinks he is. Now the bad news. The Italian bloodhound may be sniffing my trail. I think he swallowed my too tall tale too quickly."

"Hmmm. Let him follow your savoury scent to *you-know-who's* hotel. With all the grand Pooh-Bahs in town there will be hundreds of false leads for him to sniff around. That should keep him confused for a few days. After you're through with Mr. Sweet Cheques, lose the woofer and come hop across the pond."

"All righty-tighty, let the smelly eye-ties go figure and run around in circles. *Haw-haw-haw!*" said Jill in an Oscar-worthy caricature of Monty.

"I love it when you slip into character, my thwacking thespian of thrashing."

"All these extra services are going to cost you plenty, big boy. Wait 'till I slip into one of my favourite characters and dig my claws into you. I'm going to have you *my way.*"

"Be still, my fibrillating heart, and rush into my embrace, my titillating, terrorizing, heartthrob," said Karl as he snapped his cell phone shut.

Jill hung up and smiled sweetly at the portly busker. "At least he didn't lie and tell me he loves me. *Men! Oh!*"

The next day, Lou drove his old Volkswagen through heavy city traffic as Tanya navigated. The monitor of her laptop showed a city map with a flashing red dot and the occasional *PING!* as the dot changed directions.

"She's leading us around in circles," said Lou. "This has got to be some plan to keep us confused, not to lose us."

"Hang in little longer Lou," said Tanya. "We both tired after driving all long night. Looks like she stop at Excelsior Hotel maybe ten minutes now. Sorry, but signal not precise enough to identify exact spot inside hotel. Guessing west side, but cheap piece of fecal matter tracking device have no vertical dimension and big fat margin horizontal error. Lou is too frugal with other people's monies sometimes."

Lou ignored the jab at what he considered a prudent matter of parsimony. "We need to find out who she is meeting there. Can you hack in to the guest list?"

"Am already there. *Ayee, Chihuahua*, Señor Lou. Guest list read like who's who. All very rich. Best guess is Jill meeting someone at *Global Conference on the Future*. Powerful big wigs from all over world."

"We need to get someone inside that conference." Lou picked up his cell and placed a call. "Great Uncle Sergio?"

As the stereo blared Elgar's *Pomp and Circumstance*, Monty hummed along as he admired himself in the full length mirror and applied finicky finishing touches to his hair, tie, blazer, and medallions. "The sacrifices I make for the little people, the ungrateful and unwashed stinking masses," he whispered to himself. "Where's that boot-licking groveller, Lockhart, when I need him?"

The door bell to the Versailles Suite chimed, and Monty strode to the door with rising ire. "I shall have someone give him a proper thrashing, making me attend to my own attire. The very idea, expecting Royalty to feed and dress themselves."

He opened the door and said, "Now see here, Lock—"

Jill was utterly ravishing in a black suede business suit, tastefully low cut blouse, fresh coiffure, and dolphin skin attaché case.

"—hart. My word, could you be Dr. Fleming? Mr. Mucky-Pup at the PMO said to expect you, but you're so, so, yes indeedy, you certainly are."

Jill gave enough of a hint of a curtsey to push the regal buttons, but not enough to be obsequious. "I assure you, the pleasure is all mine, Your Royal Highness."

"Please, we can be less formal here. My very, very close friends call me Monty. In private, of course."

Monty gestured Jill toward a chair but she stood respectfully until his snottiness was seated. "Monty it is, then. I've been asked to help you prepare for your very, very important speech."

"Do I detect a bit of a Gloucestershire accent?"

"Worcestershire, actually. By way of Oxford, Monty." she unbutttoned her suit jacket, displaying her figure for best effect.

"Oh, my. Wooster it is."

"Well let's get started, Monty." She stroked her silky hosiery and touched Monty's sleeve with the same hand. "We must look after the speaker before we attend to the speech. Wouldn't you agree that you can't do your best work until you are totally relaxed, completely drained of every last drop of tension in your entire body, Monty?" She slid her hand from the sleeve to stroke his hand, fondling the royal knuckles.

"Oh, Wooster, oh saucy-waucy Wooster!"

Lockhart was a toad-like but impeccably dressed little man in his late 50s, who sweated profusely as he paced before a wall of human flesh in the shape of two gargantuan ex-football players turned security guards, Lamont and Cranston.

He gestured to the hotel's elevator doors and said, in a whiny British accent, "You simply must let me go up. I am the personal *valet* to His Royal Highness, for goodness sake. His butler, his major domo, his factotum, his grand *Pooh Bah!* I live to serve my betters."

"Sorry, sir, but we have strict orders. No visitors. No calls. No way. No how," said the grim-faced Lamont with no doubt or ambiguity in his voice.

Cranston added his most serious negations. "None. Nada. Zilch. Zero. Nothing. Negative. Denied. Vetoed. Overruled."

"But I have to prepare him for his big speech. His Royal Highness is quite helpless without me!"

Cranston continued in a monotone. "Leave. Take off. Disappear. Hit the road. Beat it. Scram. Take a hike."

"Perhaps, for just one second, one teensy-weensy split second?" said the cringing Lockhart.

"Cheerio. So long. *Adios. Au revoir. Joi geen. Aloha. Auf Wiedersehn. Arrivederci. Asta las vista. Da svidanya. Shalom.*"

Lockhart retreated with head down in humiliation, snivelling.

"Without so much as a goodbye."

The master bedroom in Karl's château was loosely styled after the royal chambers in the palace of Versailles. The self anointed Sun King of the 21st century had a few amenities added, including a 100" plasma HD TV on the wall opposite the bed, the king sized bed.

Karl paced back and forth in his royal blue bathrobe with ermine trim, nervously clicking the TV image on and off.

"Karl, sweetie, just leave it on and come to bed," said Mei, resplendent in a ruby nightgown, as she plucked a lump of burnt umber-coloured wax from her perfectly formed ear, using only the finest of cotton swabs imported from a genteel cotton plantation dating from the *ante-bellum* era in Alabama.

Karl continued pacing as he clicked the TV on again. A panning shot showed a large conference centre, with thousands of delegates milling about, and signs and banners representing the major non governmental organizations and most of the nations on earth. Above the stage hung a large banner, in contrasting earth tones, which read *Global Conference on the Future.*

The screen image split to show Sapphira Jones holding an ECO TV microphone.

"Good evening, everyone! This is Sapphira Jones reporting on this year's *Global Conference on the Future.* Environmental issues are always high on the agenda here, and this year the spotlight is on the recent series of epidemics. What is happening with all those plagues?! You want to know and the ECO TV news team of top notch reporters is here to give you the answer! We're hoping to get some fresh insights from distinguished scientists from leading institutions, notably representatives from the Mendel Foundation, and—sorry, excuse me."

Sapphira paused, touched her earpiece, and nodded to someone off-screen.

"I'm sorry; I have just been told that there will be a slight delay. Our keynote speaker has not yet arrived. We are looking forward to an inspiring speech from His Royal Highness—"

Karl punched the mute button. "Years of planning, the viability of the planet is at stake, and that inbred imbecile could blow it all in one night! Not to mention a lot of embarrassing questions to duck."

"Relax, relax. Your sicko psychiatrist friend can handle *you-know-who.*"

"She is twisted, but extremely talented, you must agree, my radiant ruby of randiness."

"*Kaaaarl*, you don't like her, do you? The truth!"

"Of course not, she is a mere employee, a flunky. How could you even think such a thing, O eternal flame in the cockles of my heart?" Karl turned the volume up on the TV.

Sapphira continued, finger to earpiece.

"Yes, yes. I can confirm that now. Ladies and gentlemen, I'm sorry to have to tell you this, but I've just been told the keynote speaker has suddenly become ill, and will not be joining us. Nothing too serious, just a mild case of food poisoning. Doctors suspect some sort of sauce, possibly Worcestershire."

She paused again, held up an index finger for the viewers, and looked off camera. "Yes, all right. Folks, we have some just fabulous good news! In his place, the Canadian delegates will present a panel discussion, tentatively titled 'Whence Canada? Whither Quebec? *Quo Vadis, Dominion?*' and I'm sure that it will keep all of us on the edge of our seats. And we wish a speedy recovery for His Royal Highness."

Karl raced around the room, arms upraised. "I can hear him now: '*Oh, bolly bollocks, I missed my smeggy speech!*'" he shouted in a mock Monty voice.

"Yea, Karl! You're my main man! All mine! I knew you could do it!" squealed Mei with little conical arm waves.

Karl, in his euphoria, had not looked in Mei's direction for some time. "Oh, God, Yes! Yes! Yes! I love you Ji—J—just the way you are!"

"*Aaahhh!* You said it! At last, you said it! You finally told me you love me! Ohhhh, I love the *L-word!*" Mei burst into giggles, grabbed Karl by his bathrobe belt and pulled him on top on her.

"Yes, of course, that's what I said all right. You know me; I always mean what I say." Too late to pull out some nose hairs to get the tears flowing and create the illusion of emotion.

"You are going to get lucky tonight, my love! I'm going to give you something wonderfully *special*." Mei clapped her hands twice and the lights and TV went out. In total darkness, she added, "Karl, my love, now that we're officially in love, we should get married. Now Karl, can you say the *M-word*?"

"Mmmmmmmmmmm."

Faster and more safely than shouting *FIRE!*, the announcement of a Canadian panel discussion on the future of Quebec and the Dominion cleared the thousands of delegates from the conference centre in record time.

Sergio Spenalzo and Jean Brulé moved as quickly as their age and the throng permitted. Sergio spotted his limousine less than a block away, the chauffeur lounging by the passenger door.

"Dat cretin never miss chance shoot his royal moutt off and make even bigger fool of himself, now he miss da biggest speech of his life. *Tabernac de poutine!*" said Brulé, trying to keep up with his much older companion.

"Lou tracked the mole to the Excelsior Hotel. They may still be there. Jorgensen!"

The chauffeur snapped to attention, gave a slight bow, and opened the rear door for his passengers. *Something's wrong here*, thought Sergio as they moved into traffic, *what does not add up?*

"Jorgensen, Excelsior Hotel. And Jorgensen, why are you wearing your cap in that childish fashion. That is too jejune for a ten year old."

The chauffeur turned his cap 180° to the normal position, peak over the eyes, then turned to display an evil grin worthy of a bad *Fu Man Chu* movie. "My name isn't Jorgensen, it is Mr. Chan, if you please, sir. And I will give the orders."

Chan punched a few buttons, the doors locked with a series of snaps, and the opaque, bulletproof screen rose, separating the passengers from the driver's compartment completely. With another button, he released the valve on a container of nitrous oxide, so that the last moments of two elderly Sherpas would not be entirely unpleasant.

A group of 15 Hip Hop boys in droopy pants, boxer shorts and an abundance of bling, converged on the limousine from all directions, forming an electric Eco-bike phalanx surrounding the now doomed passengers. The one nearest Sergio tapped on the window, gave a short nod of the head, and rolled the rear of his boxer shorts back enough to reveal the handle of an automatic pistol.

"Brulé, look at that, such an uncomfortable way to conceal a weapon," said Sergio with a child-like giggle.

Rising above the city din and hum of the engines, came the sound of 15 voices singing in harmony, soon joined by Mr. Chan.

> *"I don't know where, I don't know when.*
> *But I know we'll meet again . . . ."*

One of the last things Sergio Spenalzo ever saw was Lou's 1957 Volkswagen Beetle chugging along on the opposite side of the expressway.

CHAPTER 8

Only human

As the sun rose higher on the Ryuku Islands, Japan, a frail gentleman in his 90s, Kano San, returned from his morning walk to the *Ryuku Ichiban Home for Honoured Elders.* A group of elderly Japanese on the porch turned to greet him with curious glances toward the odd package he carried under one arm.

"Good morning, everyone," Kano San said to his old friends. He began to open the FPS delivery package with a little difficulty. "I am very curious about this. It's been years since someone sent old Kano a gift."

He pulled out a small radio in bubble wrap as the seniors gathered around him, and helped him remove the padding. Kano San pulled a letter from the FPS package, blew off some white powder, and wiped more powder off his hands. The seniors found more white powder on the radio, and a few of them began sneezing.

Kano San read to his friends, "You have been selected to receive a free radio with an audio recorder as part of a marketing study. Please invite your friends to listen and enjoy the pre-programmed musical selections." He picked his nose with a finger bearing the slightest trace of powder and sneezed twice, filling the air with water droplets.

Someone turned on the radio, which began to play Fats Waller's *The Joint Is Jumpin'* and the whole group began to laugh. Kano San laughed uproariously at the silly old Western music, and did a little dance, circling his friends and playfully slapping them on the back. Everyone started dancing to the infectious rhythms and slapping each other. The uniformed attendants joined in.

"I do not know why, but this old music makes me feel very good," said Kano San, licking the remnants of the white powder from his fingers, coughing and sneezing.

Soon everyone in the happy little group was coughing and sneezing, and more attendants came to their aid.

"Oh, yeah! Someone please shoot me now, I am *SO* happy!" said Kano San, just before he fell into unconsciousness.

Lou dozed in the driver's seat of his Volkswagen, his head slowly nodding forward, and finally his forehead hit the top of the steering wheel with a soft *bonk*! Fortunately, the wheel was covered with its original fluffy fleece cover, matching the teal and orange fuzzy dice which hung from the rear view mirror.

"Sorry, I drifted off, my mistake," said Lou.

"I am very sleepy also, Lou. Maybe we check news on internet, get little stimulation, *da*?" said Tanya with a great yawn.

A few taps and mouse clicks later and the image of Neville Lear came into focus, the ECO TV logo over his shoulder.

"And in the Ryuku Islands, Japan, for the third day in a row epidemics have claimed yet more lives on the third of three adjacent islands. First 10, then 20, now 30 victims have fallen to the plague in a chillingly increasing arithmetic progression. We wish to assure our viewers that there is no cause for panic. Scientific authorities from the Mendel Foundation have issued a press release on the matter, and wish to assure us that the plagues, while small but serious, are clearly further evidence of global warming and the relentless and rapacious corporate exploitation of the rainforests."

"Lou, some guy is now making big joke, laughing at us. What he do-ink next?"

"Let's think about what we can accomplish right now. Where is the signal coming from?"

"Same place. City park about two blocks from here, much open space. Would be too easy for sharp eyed Jill to spot old orange VW if we get closer."

"She's hardly moved for hours. Time to take a chance."

Lou moved into traffic and in a few minutes was at the park. "Nobody, at this hour, except the usual indigents and beggars. Let's take a walk in the park."

On a park bench a few hundred metres from the VW, Tanya narrowed the signal down to one very large, very drunk, and very smelly accordion player, an empty jug of Canadian Club whiskey still in his grasp. A sign on his accordion read *Likke reel moosek? Giv Mongo monies.* Lou kicked the end of the bench and Mongo stirred awake with a discordant B-natural fart and an F-sharp wheeze from the accordion.

"Where beautiful little lady with monies?" Mongo pulled out a new wallet with several crisp US $20 bills, and took out the tracking device. "Lady say this thing magic charm from Italian gypsies; must keep seven days to get good luck, walk seven miles each day, then throw into river while facing east and say seven times *Hail Mary.*"

"Yes, Mongo, very lucky for you, not so lucky for me." He handed Mongo a one dollar bill. Tanya scowled at Lou and added a pair of twenties.

The sky above Karl's château was dark with an approaching thunderstorm, with dark clouds anomalously moving in from the East.

Alone in the old chapel, Karl played the last few bars of the *Siegfried Idyll*, then sat in meditative silence, savouring the sweetness of his polymath genius. *Polymath?* No word could be strong enough. When his heroic journey was over, only a grand opera of his own composition, perhaps a complete cycle of seven operas in the Wagnerian style, could do his life's story justice.

DeWang approached in slippered silence, and gently coughed, the volume less than 50 decibels.

"Pardon the interruption, sir, but we believe you wished to be notified when Mr. Log-in had been prepared."

Karl rubbed his hands with glee, and clapped his factotum on the shoulder as they walked toward the centre hall. "Excellent, DeWang! And the Professor?"

"The Professor will be joining us momentarily. And, if we may so bold, sir, we believe Ms Mei Tung Nga is, uh, keenly desirous of your attention. She said something about—"

The sound of a helicopter drowned out his words. ". . . and it appears Dr. Fleming has just now arrived."

In the centre hall of the château, the mesomorphic bald dwarf, Atlas, stood on guard over a special guest. Attired in a new Eco Angels track suit, Atlas gently tapped his own chunky calf muscle with a teacher's wooden pointer, salivating in anticipation of the chance to exercise a rare opportunity to dominate.

He then wielded the pointer like a pool cue, a centre break shot to the ribs of his guest. "Wakey up, attention you must pay, incompetent hack," said Atlas in his bizarre mixture of Rumanian and Uzbek accents. "*Master* of house here is."

Woody Logan was securely if not elegantly bound to a wheelchair with a combination of police issue plastic snap-on handcuffs, and an ample layer of duct tape. He popped his head up, but could utter little more than a *Hmmph!* with a pair of Atlas's old sweat socks in his mouth. Atlas leaned in close to his prisoner and smiled broadly, revealing what was left of his yellow-brown incisors and canines, sharpened to little black points.

Karl entered from the chapel and was immediately transfixed by the vision of Mei oozing down the grand staircase in a scarlet, spandex jumpsuit that might have been applied with a spray gun, complemented by thigh-high, brilliantly polished, magenta stiletto boots from Italy. Karl admired a glimpse of his own reflection in a thigh, darkly. All fell silent at the well choreographed entrance, until she welded herself to Karl's shoulder like a seductive barnacle.

"Mei, eternal delight of my optic nerves, sparkling jewel of my crown, never has anyone in the history of the universe been remotely as stunning as you are today, supremely luminous and radiant technicolor nebula of my galaxy. May I introduce you to Mr. Woody Logan?"

Mei unglued her head from Karl's shoulder just enough to whisper, "I hear you've been asking a lot of questions, Mr. Logan. Naughty little cub reporter! Perhaps we should amputate your tongue to end your practice of 'that glib and oily art.'"

"You wouldn't dare, Dragon Lady!" shouted Woody, as defiant as he could be, speaking through the socks.

The front door opened and DeWang, bearing several matching pieces of dolphin skin luggage, followed Jill to the main hall.

Karl, the perfect host, said, "Dr. Jillian Fleming, Jill, may I introduce the grand love of my life and *élan vital* of my soul, Mei Tung Nga, and also the trusted duo of DeWang and Atlas. And last and by all means least, Mr. Woody Logan, who has the unfortunate habit of being nosy."

Jill stared into Woody's eyes and said, "You might just lose that inquisitive proboscis, Mr. Logan, sticking it into places it doesn't belong."

Woody stared back, in muffled defiance. "That's easy for you to say now, you sourpuss limey tart!"

As DeWang took Jill's bags upstairs, Karl turned toward the library, wheeling a vision in red in a parallel arc. "Mei, fragrant rose of ten thousand years of olfactory splendour, I need you, I need you to do something absolutely, vitally important for me. Our generous benefactor has been expected to call for hours now, and now I must be present for the Professor's lecture. You know how he gets if he thinks he's being ignored. Would you wait for the call in the library, my sweet, *hmmm*?"

"Karl, I must talk to you about something, I need you now, my love. *NOW?!?*"

"Right after the lecture, O precious *primum mobile* of my endocrine and limbic systems."

"OK, I'll give him the usual reassurances and flattery, and laugh at all his idiot racist remarks, but then I need your *un*-divided attention, Karl."

"Of course, my celestial siren, but you must not leave the library until he calls. Run now!" Karl gave her a wink and a squeeze of her buttocks, and Mei skipped off merrily down the hall to the library.

Karl turned back to Woody. "Fear not, Mr. Logan, you tongue and nose will be unharmed for now. We won't put you on the rack or boil you in oil. Instead, you will be treated to a very long, very detailed, lecture on—*science*."

Woody screamed through the socks, his eyes wide in terror, "No, please no! Not science, anything but that! I can stand pain, but please, not difficult concepts or long words I can't pronounce! And definitely no math, anything but math, I beg you! Mercy!"

Karl turned his attention to his other guests. "Atlas, please escort Mr. Logan to the Professor's study, and make him uncomfortable."

"Great pleasure be, Herr Doktor Master Mendel. Master-mine Herr Professor Doktor Pfizz be delight have most eager and attentive pupil, *uh-huh! uh-huh! uh-huh!*" As he wheeled the chair into the study, he gave Woody a whack on the back of the head with the pointer, and whispered, "We show you how proper respect give your betters, you, you tabloid TV video rent-boy whore." Another whack for good measure.

Professor Erik Pfizz's study was a small lecture hall, with a large, wooden desk said once to have belonged to Kaiser Wilhelm, several large wing chairs for visitors, and an array of computers, microscopes, cameras, and miscellaneous scientific equipment. Karl took centre stage while Jill waited in the doorway.

"Professor? Any time you're ready?" shouted Karl.

A small groan and an extended *"Jaaaaaaa! Mein Gott! Taschenbillard"* came from Erik's quarters adjacent to the study.

A moment later Erik emerged, a sheepskin comforter on his lap, and muttered, *"Oh, sehr gut, sehr gut,"* smoking a machine rolled marijuana cigarette.

"Woody, please grunt your greetings to Professor Erik Pfizz, my personal mentor and the greatest scientific mind of the century."

"Hello sir, pleased to meet you," said Woody through the socks.

Erik extinguished his reefer and rolled his wheelchair up to Woody. "That is Erik with a *K*, and the Pfizz is pronounced *Fizz* but spellled with a *P*; the *P* is silent, as in the swimming."

"Atlas, please ensure Mr. Logan pays very close attention to the whole lecture; there will be a very important test afterward, and a severe penalty for failure. Professor, Mr. Logan has been expressing some curiosity, and would love to hear every single detail of your work; you have all the time in the world. And he just loves mathematics."

Karl and Jill raced up the stairs two steps at a time toward the bedroom area.

Erik turned on his projector, and said to Woody, "Such an opportunity since setting the world's record for continuous lecturing at Heidelberg in 1992 I have not had. We take only the necessary short breaks for *dem Handgelenk schütteln.*"

"*Hhhmmmfff?*"

"You know, *die Handmassage? Die Onanie? Taschenbillard?*"

Woody shook his head "*No.*"

"*Old Schüttelhand?*"

Woody shook his head again.

Erik leaned in close and shouted, "Masturbation, *dummkopf!* If only the youth of today would simply make *bumsen* with mother thumb and her four daughters, we would have fewer babies and the world would not be in this terrible mess!"

Woody moved his hands the few millimetres permitted by the handcuffs, and shrugged.

"Such hopeless, mindless breeders the youth are. But back to the lecture. I have acquired much more material since 1992." Erik rubbed his hands together, cracked his neck, and took a deep, contemplative breath as a winding up exercise.

Woody gave a little groan, which earned him a whack on his ear.

"Now, Herr Logg-mann, with some ele-mentary biology we begin." On the screen, a slide showed a diagram comparing basic prokaryotic and eukaryotic cell structure. "May we ass-ume that you have never heard of the mar-vell-ous structure called, *the telomere?*"

Jill poked Karl in the ribs with a sharpened fingernail. "You are cruel, leaving that poor young man tied up and forced to listen to the old windbag. So what's the point?"

"The professor loves almost nothing more than an audience, and it gives me a cover story for my clingy Asian playmate." Karl led Jill into the master bedroom, her dolphin skin luggage already in place.

"In here? She would murder you if she knew!"

"Perfectly safe, devil girl, and think of the titillating naughtiness of it. She'll do what she's told, even if she has to sit by the phone for hours. The poor thing has a commitment fetish."

Jill started unbuttoning her blouse. "I need to change and set up some props. So you get out of here until you hear the music. Remember, you promised me if I took care of Monty, we'd do it *my way*." She slammed the door shut.

"Oh, sweet mistress of the dark side of life, at last I've found you!"

Karl rushed back to Erik's study and took the nearest seat, feigning intense interest in the lecture. Erik was smoking another reefer with one hand, wielding a green laser pointer with the other. The screen showed a map illustrating the effects of global warming.

"And you say you are the journalist, the superficial tele-vision journ-alist who tells the old ladies and little children to recycle and drive the small car and all will be well. *Fooey!* Do you know how close we are to the point of the ir-reversible damage due to the climate change, the loss of the species, burning the rainforests? *Ja!* These and many more things we will in micro-scopic detail examine."

Atlas took a whack at Woody's kneecap for a change, shattering the pointer.

"Marvellous!" said Woody in his sock voice, "great lecture, sir."

"Wonderful lecture, Professor, I'll be right back," said Karl as he bolted down the hall toward the library.

Mei sat in the chair nearest the speakerphone, reading aloud from *King Lear*. "Where was I? 'You shall be *ours*. Natures of such deep trust we shall much need. *You* we first *seize* on.' Oh, yes, yes, yes!"

The door popped open and Mei flung herself onto the table. "Karl! Seize me! Right here and now, the time is right."

"The time is always right, my punctual pussycat. Has you-know-who called?"

"No. Karl, I've got to have you right now! I'm so horny I think I'm going crazy for you. It must be my cycle, or the excitement of the big day, or something, please Karl, do it to me right now, just do it! I want to be Mother Earth to your Father Sky. Unzip your lightning bolt, and zap me, big boy!" She began to unzip one magenta boot.

Karl's eyes lit up, following the tantalizing track of her zipper. "Ah, oh my gosh, you want to—*hmmm*—you're all ready to make the beast of two backs. And right on top of the *fail*—well, you know how I love a surprise!"

The sounds of the opening bars of the William Tell Overture beckoned.

"*Ahh!* The Professor! *Aaa-Haa!* That's, uh, that's the theme music to the most crucial part of his lecture. I can't miss it, O rhyme of my Rubaiyat!"

Karl bolted, slammed the door, and opened it again. "But hold that thought, Earth Goddess, I shall return."

Mei scowled at the door, zipped her boot back up, rolled off the table and went back to *King Lear*.

Erik leaned toward Woody as close as he could, their wheelchairs butting.

"So! Obvious, is it not, to even a *dummkopf* like you that it is simply a matter of Darwinian evolution, that we have been so successful as the species, that the *root cause* of the imminent destruction of the planet is simply *TOO MANY PEOPLE!?!"*

Karl poked his head into the room and shouted, "Bravo, Professor Pfizz, bravo!" and disappeared again.

Karl screeched to a stop at the master bedroom, almost tripping over Jill's shoes outside the slightly opened door. As he jumped in and flung off his jacket with a flourish, a nylon rope lariat fell over his shoulders and snapped tight, pinning his arms. Jill moved behind him, planted her knee in his lumbar spine and tightened the lariat with all her strength, then knotted the rope around his hands, securing them behind his back. She ripped his shirt from his shoulders and spun him around so that Karl could take in the sight of her, entirely in black, with a cowboy's ten gallon hat, eye mask, leather vest with a sheriff's badge, chaps, and cowboy boots.

She grabbed the rope and roughly dragged him to the bed. With a cinematic Western accent, she drawled, "Hop on, pardner, it's round up time. Maybe I'll brand yuh with mah *Big J* branding iron, before ah strings yuh up." She pushed him onto the bed and straddled him, holding onto the rope.

"Ya-hoo!" shouted Karl over the music. "Ride me into the sunset, cowgirl!"

Mei's reading of the great Shakespearean tragedy was soon interrupted by what sounded like a female voice shouting *Hi-Ho-Sil-Sil-ver* over the din of the music. She put her *King Lear* on the table and rushed down the hall to Erik's study. She poked her head inside, just as Erik was reaching a frothing at the mouth, eye rolling, oratorical peak.

"So! We must the population quickly reduce, and save the planet before it is totally destroyed. At eight billion people we are now at the tipping point of total annihilation. That is the whole intention, *ja*? Yes? *Yes*?"

From upstairs came the same female voice, shouting a primal *Yes! Yes! Oh, God Yes! Yaa Hoo! Yaa Hoo!!* followed by a guttural masculine *Yee-Hawww!*

Mei gasped in horror. "Karl!?"

Erik, Woody and Atlas simultaneously looked upstairs.

"Kaaa-rrr-lll! Poor thing, Karl baby, what's happening to you?!?" Mei bleated as she leapt up the staircase toward the bedroom as fast as her stiletto boots would allow.

The William Tell Overture reached its climax with a grand crescendo. Jill was riding Karl like a Brahma bull, nearing the eight minute mark of a championship rodeo performance, when the door burst open.

Jill broke the awkward silence. "Whoa there, hoss, we got trouble. Redskins!!"

Karl's head was by now dangling over the edge of the bed, upside down. He first saw the magenta boots, the scarlet jumpsuit, and finally, the upside down face of a woman scorned.

"Inverted sugar of my sweetest desserts! Reddest redskin of my wild west wet dreams!"

"Don't, just don't, you, you," she hissed and slammed the door. Standing outside she saw Jill's shoes, tried to scream, but could only gasp for air.

Karl's voice whimpered through the door. "Mei? Please, I'm sorry, I'm. I'm . . ."

"A knave, a rascal, an eater of broken meats, a base, proud, shallow, beggarly, three-suited, hundred-pound, filthy worsted-stocking knave; . . ."

Holding on to the walls and then the railing for support, she staggered along the hall and down the stairs, the well known speech from *King Lear* coming to her lips effortlessly.

". . . a lily-livered, action-taking knave; a whoreson, glass-gazing, superfinical rogue; one-trunk-inheriting slave; . . ."

She was oblivious to DeWang, polishing the gargoyles on the banister posts, who discreetly pretended to ignore her.

". . . one that wouldst be a bawd in way of good service, and art nothing but the composition of a knave, . . ."

She wandered into the study. Erik, Atlas and Woody wisely ignored her.

". . . beggar, coward, pander, and the son and heir of a mongrel bitch,"

Karl raced down the stairs to the study, wearing only a towel.

". . . whom I will beat into a clamorous whining, if thou deny the least syllable of the addition." She moved in her daze toward the main door.

Karl tried his most pleading, pathetic and desperate snivel. "Mei, I love you! I just said the L-word. Does that mean nothing to you?"

She snapped around faster than the strike of a serpent's tooth. "Love? *Love?!?* You don't know the meaning of the word, you heartless vacuum tube! You suppurating, festering, pestilent carbuncle!"

"Forgive me! *Please!* I'm only human, sweetie pie. I—I can't help myself—I'm just like everybody else, I have an uncontrollable sex drive that trumps my cognitive capacity. It's in my genes!"

Mei stormed out, slamming the door in his face.

Rain fell in torrents down her face, rain in lieu of tears which would not flow. A bolt of lightning and a long roar of thunder transformed a once sweetly selfish face from a stunned, blank, neutrality to a hateful visage that would have struck fear into the heart of Satan.

"Revenge."

CHAPTER 9

A once-in-a-lifetime experience

The hum of activity at *The Global Headquarters of the Mendel Foundation for Ecological Research and Education* had increased several decibels over the last few days. As Earth Day approached, the big board now read:

WORLD POPULATION:
7,999,342,466
COUNTDOWN TO EARTH DAY, NOON GMT:
72 hours 1 min. 3 sec.
PLEDGED PARTICIPANTS ~ GLOBAL TOTAL:
6,748,801,609

Now on her feet for 12 hours and ready for a break, Sheila contemplated the choice of fair trade Columbian coffee, harvested by former Medellin prostitutes now working in a drug addicts' rehabilitation program; or, pre-industrial, pollution free, ice-age glacial water from the Penny Ice Cap, bottled in Pangnirtung, Nunavut, by an Inuit community-owned not-for-profit corporation; or, freshly squeezed orange juice, made with oranges from a workers' cooperative in Valencia, Spain, which hired physically and mentally handicapped women immigrants and refugees. After a moment's torment trying to make the most politically correct choice, she snapped up all three and plunked into her chair to watch the nearest plasma screen.

"*Oy!* Mates! Heads up, everyone, it's the new commercial!" A crowd of fatigued Eco Angels gathered around Sheila; Ndugu and Iqbal snuggled in close to her ample breasts for a coffee break *à trois*.

On screen, Cookie Lemon dominated the camera with her perfectly icy blue eyes, sun-kissed long blond hair, and wearing a string of black Tahitian pearls, a grass skirt, and an oyster shell and braided grass top. And oil, the finest olive oil carefully kneaded into every pore of her firm flesh by a team of loyal and vigilant volunteers. Behind her, several hypnotically attractive Eco Angels from all over the globe, attired in the new designer track suits, played volleyball and cavorted with the nearly naked, athletic local natives, all set in a lush Pacific island paradise. A goal was scored, and they all cheered and converged on Cookie for a demonstrably affectionate, 20 person group hug, laughing, cavorting and kissing each other playfully, as a perfect sunset illuminated the sky and ocean.

Cookie held up her ECO TV microphone and spoke directly to the camera. "Hi everyone! Did you know there's still time to join the Eco Angels and be a *Group Hug Leader* on Earth Day? Come on and join us, and we'll show the world how much *love* there is in your heart, and help save the planet. All expenses will be paid by the Mendel Foundation, and life experience school credits at all levels are available from the Mendel Institute of Technology. We would just *love* to have *you join us* for the most amazing, awesome, totally brilliant *once-in-a-lifetime* experience." Cookie and the others melded their perfect bodies together, all 40 sparkling eyes and 640 perfect, sparkling white teeth gleaming for the camera, as the earth toned captions appeared on the screen:

Visit the Eco Angels website: www.sharethelove.karl
Call: 1 888 BIG LOVE

Back at the Foundation, before the screen could fade to black, every telephone in the building started ringing. The Eco Angels burst into a deafening cheer and rushed to their places to start taking calls.

A vintage jeep pulled away from a village on the outskirts of the city of Ferkessédougou in West Africa. Kimberly, Ganesh and Pong looked at each other and then at what was supposed to be their pup tent, a sagging canvas structure suspended by a nylon rope, and with torn mosquito netting crudely patched with duct tape. Several local children stopped playing with a deflated soccer ball to stare at the strange trio. Kimberly snuggled up to Ganesh, who pulled a wrinkled sheet of paper from his backpack.

"It says to ' . . . spend the time between now and Earth Day getting to know the local people, play games, sing songs, and above all practice group hugs so that everyone in the whole world will be hugging their neighbours and loved ones at the same time. Love, kisses, and hugs, Karl. P.S. The new uniforms will be sent by parachute. Don't open the plastic wrappings until noon on Earth Day! *X O X O X* K.' That's about it, guys."

Kimberly slid her hand down to Ganesh's butt, and said to Pong, "We're going to go visit the locals, maybe practice some hugging or whatever, so can you, like, fix up the tent, or do whatever?"

Pong glanced at the tent and said, "Sure, take off, go and hug, frolic, do whatever, wherever, whenever." Kimberly and Ganesh sprinted into the nearby fern-like bushes, pulling off their t-shirts on the way.

"Share the love. Check. Earn school credits. Check. See the world. Check." Pong untied the rope from the tent, and began to fashion a hangman's noose at one end.

The local native children gathered closer and giggled when the bushes began to move, and then speak in a strange tongue. "*Aaaaaaa hooooo!* Yes! Oh, Yes, Ganesh, make me a big momma! I want all your babies! *Whooooaaaaahhhh!*"

"Watch the college kids run off to the *banga banga* bushes. Check. Listen to the college kids go *banga banga* all night long. Check."

The children circled the bushes laughing and pointing, paying no attention to Pong.

"Have your parents swallow the biggest load of horse manure the world has seen since Hercules cleaned the Augean stables. Check. Let them push me into this idiotic enterprise so they can tell their friends little Pong is an Eco Angel, too, and so cute they put Pong on the boob tube as a pawn in who knows what fecal brained plan to make an even bigger mess of the world than it already is. Check. Share the love? What love, it's all a big con job, all lies. Abandon last vestige of hope that the world is anything but completely psychotic, we are all doomed to suffer and die, and things will never get better only worse. Check. End it all today. Check."

Pong proceeded to climb the nearest sturdy tree, noose in hand.

The *Pangaea Landfill Site* was created almost a century ago, on the site of a defunct open pit coal mine. Decade after decade of unprocessed urban waste filled the pit and extended beyond the original boundaries to several connecting valleys. An unintended consequence was that the site had become a toxic waste factory, creating rivulets of chemical and biological poisons, heavy metals, unknown toxic chemical compounds and pathogenic micro-organisms, all leaching into the local aquifer and proven to have contaminated the state's water supply. Meanwhile, aerobic and anaerobic bacteria continue to convert organic waste into the greenhouse gases carbon dioxide and methane. Environmental groups such as *The Clean Water Confluence* and *Vegans for Zero Waste* had successfully lobbied for the closure of the site, leaving it idle since the late 20ᵗʰ century as the political and legal battles continued. One unintended consequence was that household and industrial waste then had to be carried by an armada of trucks to a similar dump in an adjacent state, where free enterprise is sacred and freedom reigns, and where the same pollutants percolate into another branch of the same aquifer.

Another unintended consequence of the closure is that the *Pangaea* site became a convenient dumping ground for environmentally uncaring and unsophisticated criminal organizations to dispose of some former enemies and other surplus humans.

Lou stood near the edge of a small mountain of filth, a handkerchief over his nose. On this morning, the only sounds came from a flock of circling seagulls and the rustle of rats in the rubble.

"Is awful, Lou, I never before smell such thing." Even Tanya had lost her nerve today, as she huddled behind Lou. Luciano, Lucia, and the twins stood a few paces away, averting their eyes. Luciano wept silently.

Lou nodded to Mario, who pulled back a filthy canvas sheet, revealing the bodies of Sergio Spenalzo and Jean Brulé. They had been dead long enough now to acquire a gray-green colour, and were beginning to bloat from the microbial maelstrom occurring within their now helpless innards. Flies were congregating and laying eggs in their flesh, and a few brave seagulls flew in closer, in anticipation of an easy and nutritious banquet to follow, starting with the decaying eyeballs, considered a delicacy by scavengers.

"This is all my fault," said Lou. "If I hadn't gotten them directly involved, they would not be here. I should have seen the danger. I was so stupid, stupid, stupid."

Tanya came closer and rubbed Lou's shoulder. "I know is very difficult, but important to focus, now."

Lou took a deep breath through the handkerchief, put on a pair of latex gloves and began to examine the bodies. "No personal effects, identification, or money left. Each was shot at least a dozen times. The bullet holes in the chest and head are starting to deteriorate, but the pattern suggests high calibre automatic pistols, like the ones in the underground garage. With the warmer temperatures this year decomposition is proceeding more rapidly than usual. Their colour suggests not only the normal putrefaction but also opportunistic bacterial and fungal infections of the epidermis, not surprising considering the present location. At least we can be grateful they died quickly, no evidence of bruising or lacerations about the hands, faces, necks, or—what the blazes?"

The others gathered closer as Lou gingerly inserted his latex finger into the mouth of his late, great uncle, and pulled out a small square of paper. He read in a monotone, "Life is short, death is long, and it's later than you think. Enjoy yourself, for goodness' sake, while you're still looking pink." A single tear rolled down Lou's still pink cheek.

Tanya took Lou's arm and said, "We can do forensic test, ballistics, maybe trace paper, find some clue like fingerprints."

Luciano picked up the cue. "Sure, I'm gonna send out all-a the boys, they gonna ask around, put on a bit-a pressure, and we gonna find some squeaky guy and Enrico and Mario gonna sit on him and-a make him sing like-a the canary, eh boys?"

Lou took off the gloves and pitched them into a puddle of polluted water. "Don't you get it? Any of you? This was our last chance. Herb is dead, the mole is gone, our two best contacts died trying to help us. No more clues. No leads. There is nowhere to go from here. In a few days, all of us are going to look just like them, all bloated and rotting and stinking, every colour but pink. We lost. He won. Now he can sit back and laugh at us and our feeble efforts to find the madman who is about to exterminate billions of people. And no one on earth can stop him."

Lou yanked his old wooden office window up as far as it would go, and sat on the sill to enjoy the glowing sunset in the evening smog. Even at this late hour the traffic was heavy, with an almost contiguous mass of filthy cars, trucks and buses competing for road room and filling the air with petrochemical waste. An absurdly long limousine stood out from the pack as it circled the block for the second or third time, trying to find a double parking space. On the sidewalk below him were the usual throngs of pedestrians, kids on skateboards, and buskers and panhandlers plying their trades. In nearby alleys and doorways, neighbourhood indigents curled up with their evening snifters of fortified wine. It occurred to Lou that the situation was something like that of a large asteroid headed for an inevitable dead centre collision with planet earth. *Why tell them what's going to happen to them all? How could a few days of panic help anything?*

Tanya tapped on her computer furiously, because that was what she knew how to do best. "World about to come in dramatic ending and CIA have nothing show for billion dollar effort. MI6 nothing. Interpol *nyet*. Canadian intelligence still holding entire staff like prisoner in hotels, for court ordered multicultural sensitivity training and aboriginal rights workshops."

Lou sat beside her at the table, idly playing with a fly casting fishing rod. "Don't waste your time."

"CDC and Winnipeg still trying do DNA sequence from Japan samples, but molecular structure keep breaking down too quickly. Same thing at USAMRIID and other top labs, but no lucky strikes anywhere."

"At best that would give us some detail, not who or where or when. Who *is* this guy? Does he never, ever make a mistake?" Lou took a few pills, washed them down with cold coffee, and rubbed the back of his neck.

"Headache again, Lou? Feeling depressed?"

"Depressed? No, just a bit tense. You know, Tanya, I'm beginning to feel a bit ambivalent about the whole thing. Sometimes I even get the dark idea that the best thing for the world would be for him to win, knock off a few billion people, and at least give a few other species a chance to survive. Why should every other species have to pay for humanity's excesses? Did you know that the rate of species loss is higher now than at any other time in the planet's history, even higher than the Permian-Triassic or the Cetacious-Tertiary extinctions?"

"I think you say this maybe seven or eight times in last month. Sound vaguely familiar."

"Look at what we do, killing the rhinoceros for their horns, black bears for their gall bladders, all for idiotic folk remedies of no value. We destroy habitat and directly or indirectly, killing sturgeons, eels, and tigers."

"Lou, what are you talking about? Is not relevant to solving problem."

"Sorry, I'm rambling, aren't I? But think about it for a minute. We take over animal habitats to make room for the rapacious expansion of human habitat, and where does it end? At what point do we say the lives of the few remaining tigers are worth at least as much as the humans who would occupy their turf? Is there no ethical calculus to tell us when to stop bloating human numbers at the cost of every other creature that stands in our way?"

"Is stinking thinking, Lou. Must work from assumption saving billions people is good think. No brainer, *da?*"

"Sure, no brainer, slam dunk, axiomatic and syllogistic, self evident, a truth universally acknowledged, *eros* versus *thanatos*, will to live and all that. Live people good, dead people bad. Q.E.D., P.D.Q., and R.I.P."

"Huh?"

"It doesn't matter, I'm just thinking aloud. Nothing matters anymore. The world is mad and we're all going to die."

Lou put the fishing rod back and picked up his favourite trophy, the barracuda, and set it on the table in front of him. "Maybe I'll go fishing, so I can die on my boat. Anything but sitting around waiting for the plague to kill me slowly. Maybe I'll go hug a manta ray for Earth Day and end it all quickly before the big pandemic hits. Maybe I'll steal your jug of vodka (that I'm not supposed to know about) from your filing cabinet drawer labelled 'Spiritual Studies,' chug it down with a handful of tranquillizers (wasn't that nice of the mental hospital to give me a very large supply) and lie down in the freezer in my Uncle Franco's butcher shop. Maybe I'll just take Uncle Luciano's pistol and fire one shot into my brainstem, that would do it. Maybe I'll go to the zoo, pole vault into the snake pit and duke it out with the King Cobra or the Anaconda. That should finish me off in less than three minutes. Then you can have my remains burned and scattered, with no trace left of my existence. On the other hand, have me buried for worm food, throw me in a hole with all the other useless garbage, and set up a stone bearing my famous last words, *On the Whole I Would Rather Have Aborted This Mission.*"

"Lou, cannot take this."

"Nothing now but death, horror, pestilence, meaninglessness, utter bleak absurdity, abysmal ignorance. Complete extinction of an anathematic life. Nothing to look forward to but an eternal cycle of madness and death in a completely amoral, godless, uncaring universe. And then the void, the eternal unconscious emptiness to which all of us have been aspiring with every thought, word, and deed; the singularity *sans sensation* where time and space, faith, hope and charity, no longer exist, the dark oblivion of non-existence that awaits every last, doomed, condemned, damned one of us."

"We're done here." Tanya snapped her laptop shut, gathered her belongings, and headed to the door, lightly touching Lou on the shoulder. "If you can, please to join us at Antonio's, maybe you feel better with family around."

Lou simply nodded without looking at her. She tiptoed out, leaving the door slightly ajar. He clicked the TV on and watched the Eco Angels commercial with Cookie Lemon. *Hugs and love to save the world. What kind of fools would believe such naive nonsense. Poor kids, if they only knew.*

Lou clicked the TV off, picked up a fishing magazine and went back to sit on the window sill, aimlessly flipping the pages and watching the passing parade. The sun was now below the horizon, the city colour changing to twilight, the office darkening.

Minutes later, a light footstep in the hall first broke Lou's reverie. Then an extended *squeeeeeeeeek* as the door slowly opened and the hall light flooded in. He turned, still sitting on the window sill.

Mei Tung Nga stood in the door frame, backlit by the hall light, wearing a simple black evening dress, diamond choker, fishnet opera gloves and stockings. She slowly scanned the office contents before locking eyes with Lou.

"I should have guessed you were a fisherman. Are you a fisherman?"

"Sorry, is it the smell?"

"You've been looking for the great, big, bad fish, the biggest and baddest fish in the world."

Lou nodded once, not losing eye contact.

"And you've been coming up empty, every time, haven't you?"

Nod.

"The problem is, you've been casting your net in the wrong waters. You have to know *where* to fish to catch the great, white shark at the end of the world. Would you like me to show you, Luigi?"

"Call me Lou. Please."

CHAPTER 10

Share the love

"KARL MENDEL!?!"

Mei led Lou into her posh suite at the Excelsior Hotel and turned on one soft, romantic light.

"You have got to be kidding me! Karl Mendel? This cannot be," said Lou, "Karl Mendel is the most popular guy on the planet, Mr. Save the World."

"Of course," said Mei, opening the well stocked mini bar. She poured herself a fine white wine in a thin stemmed glass, and gestured for Lou to help himself. "It's a great cover. He's made himself bullet proof. Just try to accuse him of anything and the world will laugh in your face. And he gets young idealists all over the globe to do all his donkey work. Useful idiots, he calls them."

"The Eco Angels? How do they fit in?"

"Look, how do you wipe out more than six billion people so fast no one can figure it out until it's too late? The organizational and logistics problems are phenomenal. *Hmmm*, how about a global group hug, everyone '*sharing the love*' all around the world at the same time? Love me, love my freshly manufactured track suit from North Korea crawling with freshly manufactured germs."

"Then North Korea becomes the bad guy who takes the rap if it ever gets out. No one would have any trouble believing that one." Lou poured himself a ginger ale, a large ginger ale with ice. "Now that I think of it, whenever Karl speaks there never is much substance."

"Karl? Substance? C'mon, Lou, you sell the sizzle, not the steak. Substance, now that is funny. Wait until I tell the Professor. Substance." She added a cute little *hee-hee* chortle.

"The thing I will never understand is how patently phony people like Karl can seem so attractive to people. He has phenomenal charisma, charm, call it what you will. Not to digress, Mei, but another thing: Karl seems to have a lot of success in, you know, attracting, uh, well heck, how does he get to be so gosh darned irresistible to women?"

Mei snapped the stem of her glass, and fixed herself another drink. "OK, here it is, the full story, Lou, but then *puh-lease* no more about charming Karl and his women. First and foremost, he's got a lot of natural talent, that's why the conspirators chose him as their front man. He's been prepared and groomed for years to become Mr. Selfless Saviour just when the world is ripe for his act, and that's a perfect 'good boy' routine that makes people feel safe with him. He's got phenomenal natural energy and infectious enthusiasm. But if there is such a thing as charismatic engineering, he's had it all. He has a team of specialists coordinating everything around him for maximum psychological impact. He's had plastic surgery to polish his nearly perfect, natural good looks, liposuction, cosmetic dentistry with the finest veneers glued onto his old yellow fangs, coloured contact lenses, all that stuff, thousands of hours of training in acting, fashion, dance, voice lessons, coaching from the best psychologists in the world, all of that and more. Oh, yeah, and the best hairpiece money can buy."

"A hairpiece! I just knew that guy was wearing a rug." Lou ran his fingers through his thinning hair.

Mei smiled and said, "Yes, Karl Mr. 'Perfect' Mendel is having a bad hair decade. Lou, you probably stick to the facts, and ignore feelings, and like most people, you never think of all of this charismatic management consciously, so he gets to fly below the radar."

"Emotional intelligence," said Lou, "that was always my blind spot."

Mei swallowed her drink and stared at Lou. "You want to know about Karl and all the women you see him with on TV? Don't look at the content of the conversation, that's largely scripted in advance. Look at the whole picture. The manipulator is the message. Beneath the manners of a dancing school master lie the morals of a whore. He wins, he always wins and he doesn't care how he wins."

"Got it. He's a sociopath."

"More likely a psychopath and the world's biggest narcissist. I don't know if Karl is capable of loving anyone but Karl, that megalomaniac, mesmerizing Svengali. He can cast a spell on anybody, and is more seductive than Count Dracula. Once you've let him get to you, if you let your defences down, he chews away at your insides, devours your soul, sucks out your free will, until you can't think of living your life without him. I love him so much I hate him to pieces."

"Wow! And so that's how he gets all those women?"

"Lou, in some ways you're more emotionally dense and less sensitive than a brain damaged autistic ox. Sorry, that was rude. Hang on, there's more. The master stroke. He had a special cologne engineered for his use only, designed to work with his unique body chemistry. It smells like the ordinary $2,000 an ounce stuff that everyone wears, but what you can't smell consciously are the pheromones, chemical signals that animals give off to potential mates to indicate they are in the rutting season and ready to *rock 'n' roll*. Trust me, it works. It feels like an invisible emotional avalanche and once you get a whiff you are doomed, you have absolutely no resistance, and he could make you play fetch and jump through hoops of fire if he wanted to. And it not only works on women and gay boys, even straight men are affected to some extent. Did you see that nerdy twerp who interviewed him in Paris? Snivelling and hugging Karl, gassing on about love and saving the world? All chemistry, all subconscious. Hit enough people like that directly, especially on TV, then mass hysteria sets in and the whole world is in love with you, and they don't know why. The more people who love you madly the more people will fall in love with you. The frenzy just grows and grows like a giant snowball, and now he's got billions of people in love with him."

"Wow. Love really is blind, isn't it?"

"One last thing. You know all those women interviewers who are all over him? Always young and healthy women? Karl would never admit it to me, but I found out from his mentor, Professor Pfizz, that he has a team of investigators track their menstrual cycles—"

"Now that's ridiculous!" said Lou. "How could they possibly find out, when, you know."

"Ever hear of investigators going through someone else's garbage? Young, healthy, fertile women? Do you need more details, Lou?"

"No, thank you. Too much information. I get it now."

"So they track all that messy stuff, and then Karl insists he can only do the show on the day which happens to be at the peak of their fertility when they are naturally at their horniest, ready for a fumble and a tumble, and just craving a bit of the old in-and-out. Then he walks in on the peak day, drenched in cologne giving off a monsoon of pheromones, flashes his sparkling eyes and teeth—"

"And his hairpiece," said Lou, clenching his ginger ale.

"And his hairpiece, sweet talk, and his 'I love you madly and want you to bear all my children' look, and the girls are devasted, and he looks like the greatest guy in the world on the boob tube. The only people it doesn't work on are those with a rare genetic disorder rendering them completely asexual."

Lou paused in thought. "I'm totally flabbergasted. The whole plan has been carefully engineered in every way, scientifically, socially, and even emotionally. He's hit us in all of our blind spots."

Mei swallowed her drink, looked at Lou with a sly smile, and said, "Excuse me while I freshen up for a minute," and disappeared into the bathroom.

Lou sat on the edge of the bed, head in hands, trying to absorb the enormity of what he had just learned.

A few minutes later, Mei emerged in a diaphanous black nightgown, posed against the door frame, and said, "So tell me, Lou, how do you like *my* perfume?"

The sweet notes of *O, mio babbino caro* flowed from Magda's violin as she tried to console the downcast guests at Antonio's bar. Enrico, Mario and Lucia were gobbling chips and pretzels at the far end, watching TV, as Tanya waved to Antonio.

"Vodka martini. Doubles."

"Whoa, whoa, take it-a easy, beautiful lady," said Luciano, putting his arm around her. "That stuff canna kill you." Antonio placed the martini in front of her.

"Sorry, am worried about Lou. He take troubles of worlds onto shoulders."

"Hey, he's-a been through plenty-a tough-a time before. He's gonna be OK."

"Not like this, so bitter, and helpless. And he is so lonely." She snapped back about half of her drink. "And now we are here having nice drinks, beautiful music, good friends, and he is all by himself with fate of world at stake." She gulped the rest of her martini and held up two fingers to Antonio.

"Alone, all alone."

Magda switched tunes and played *Alone!* for Tanya, who was losing count of the number of double vodka martinis she had consumed. Or were they triples? Enrico nudged Mario and gestured up to the TV. "More people dead from this disease stuff in Japan. That's awful."

"Yeah, it seems to be all over the world," said Mario. "Hey, Magda, how about some happy music?" A big smile erupted on Magda's face and she began to play *Enjoy yourself.*

Luciano smacked Mario on the head. "Hey! This is serious! And look at this poor girl, so sad." Magda went back to playing *Alone!* Luciano put his arm around Tanya and kissed her on the forehead. "You tell Uncle Luciano all about it."

Tears flowed down her cheeks and into the glass, mercifully diluting the vodka. "Nothing we can do. Whole world is doomed. Lou right. World is mad and we all going die."

Tanya's stomach rumbled, then the rumble moved north. Luciano looked at her anticipating the worst and Antonio reached for an empty ice bucket. Tanya pursed her pretty lips and emitted a long, loud *EEEUUURRRPPP!!!* Fortunately no food solids or fluids accompanied the belch, and Luciano relaxed a little. She finished her drink and ordered again.

"We sit here and have nice little party and leave Lou all alone. He find it so hard to be close to people. Nobody can reach him. Luciano, what we do?"

"Maybe we gonna pray for poor, sad Luigi, all by himself tonight, in his loneliness."

The Ride of the Valkyries boomed from the hotel's compact stereo.

"Wagner, I should have guessed," said Lou.

Mei started to unbutton his shirt and pulled at his chest hair with her teeth. "Ouch!" said Lou, "Nothing rough, please."

"I don't like it rough, either. Karl likes it rough with that kinky psychiatrist."

"Aha! I knew it."

Mei gave him a deep French kiss to take his mind off her rival.

"Aah, ah, ooh, that feels good," said Lou.

He began kissing her neck. "And the big day, when is the big bug going to be released?"

"The big one, mmmm, very big. Earth Day, all planned around the global group hug. The new uniforms won't be delivered until just before noon GMT. Once it starts it will spread like wildfire, then people start to panic and run, and it spreads even faster." She reached to unbutton his pants, fumbling around in the dark. "Holy mackerel! Lou, you are as hard as a *rock!"*

Lou looked puzzled for a second, then said, "Oh, sorry, that really is a pistol in my pocket. My uncle insisted I carry this little 9 mm, but I'm not at all comfortable with it." He pulled out the pistol, checked the safety, and set it carefully on the dresser, and a little look of relief crept into his face. "But I am truly glad, I am very, very, sincerely glad to see you."

Lou took her in his arms again. "Who knows about all of this, besides Karl?"

Mei now had his shirt off and ran her fingers through his hair. "Only a few close conspirators know the whole picture, and a few technicians in the lab know all the technical stuff. The bug burns itself out quickly and the whole shebang should be over in a few days."

"Billions dead, in days, that's unthinkable."

"But we'll survive, won't we Lou, we're a team now, aren't we, Lou? Committed? Two hearts beating as one? Pumping together?"

"Ouch! Gently, gently. Where is the lab, exactly, the one with the pathogens?"

"French Alps, his château near the Swiss border. Do you believe in monogamy, Lou, true love, joined together forever? Committed?"

"France, love France. Do you know the address?"

"Mendel Labs. Try the Yellow Pages. Hello? Commitment? Monogamy?" Mei took a firm grasp of the situation.

"Yes, oh, gosh that feels so good, right on *tARget!* Monogamy, Mmmmm. Interesting anthropological concept."

"We'll show him Lou, oh yes, you can blow up all his stupid plans and save the world, that'll teach that two timing lecher! Blow him up, Lou!"

"Blow, yes, very sooooon. How do we blow him up exactly?"

"He has a big weakness, two, in fact, if you count his inability to keep his paws off other women. The failsafe device. If he thinks the jig is up he can blow up the lab, kill all the pathogens, and all the evidence is destroyed. Then he blames the animal liberation psycho fringe or someone like that, and he's still Mr. Squeaky Clean. That squeaky, filthy rat! Oh, god, Lou, you're huge!"

"It must be the Italian in me."

"Let's blow him up now, Lou! Lou! You swine!"

"Swine? Who, me?"

"Not you, Karl. He's the twisted little swine! Lou, you're the blue ribbon giant champion Clydesdale of my dreams. You make my body want to sing, sing like a Valkyrie, Lou, Lou!"

"Oh, yes, it's been years. so good, good, good."

"We're a team now, Lou. Committed. Come with me, together. Commitment! Say it, Lou, say the C-word!"

"Certainly!"

The Ride of the Valkyries was reaching its crescendo at the same time as Mei and Lou. She dug her exquisitely manicured nails into Lou's back and shouted, "Oh God, yes! YES! I hate you! I HATE YOU KARL!!"

"Call me Lou, *pleeeeeeeeease!*"

143

Magda escorted the distinguished party to the parking lot with the sweet strains of *The Party's Over*. Luciano and Lucia supported Tanya, staggering, sobbing and snivelling.

"Luciano, *tovarisch*, I love you all so much."

"Just take-a some deep breath, you gonna feel-a better," said the avuncular Luciano. "Nice cool air, good for you, eh?"

He steered Tanya toward a large garbage pail near the rear exit of Antonio's, and whispered, "Lucia, you gonna step back a bit," and gestured in a circular arc not intended to represent a rainbow.

"Big plague all over big world. PLAGUE! *Da*? Kaputski. All gonna die, like old guys in dump. Even nice Uncle Lush-a-now." She squeezed his cheeks into a kissy face, tried to plant one on his lips and missed by several inches.

Luciano was rescued by the sound of a limousine smoothly rolling to a stop only a few steps away. Enrico and Mario prepared to pull out their pistols.

Lou stepped out first, and assisted Mei in her graceful entrance.

Lou broke the stunned silence. "We're back in business, and with this beautiful lady's help, we can stop him. Everyone, say hello to May Tung Yah!"

Another round of introductions with impeccable manners. *Nice to meet you. A pleasure. Enchanté. Love the gown. You're all so nice.*

The mood was shattered by a cossack-like bellow from near the garbage cans. "Say hello to WHO, Loo-eee-gee?"

Lou took Mei's arm and escorted her to meet Tanya. He pronounced her name carefully. "May, Tung, Yah."

"Well, you can go tongue your—" and a perfectly formed stream of vodka with a chaser of stomach acids and mucous took a perfect parabolic path to the dead centre of the garbage can, all in accord with Newton's laws of motion.

"The pleasure is all mine," said Mei in her best PR voice, extending an elegant, gloved hand.

Lou rushed over to support his suffering colleague. "Tanya, you look terrible!"

Tanya looked at Mei and then at Lou in disbelief. "Lou, you didn't, did you? With *her?* You couldn't! You wouldn't?"

Lou gave a sheepish shrug, and the rest of the group feigned interest in the night sky.

"Lou, how could you?"

"I, I, . . . I closed my eyes and thought of Canada."

CHAPTER 11

Earth Day minus 2: Comeuppance Day

Karl wiped the sweat from his brow with a fresh tissue, and removed the last of six screws securing the failsafe device from a hidden compartment beneath the speakerphone in his library. He gingerly placed a small beanbag on top, adding a few ounces of pressure to dampen any vibrations, slid his screwdriver under each of the four corners to loosen any adhesion, and then slowly lifted the entire apparatus up and turned it over. Gently flashing red LEDs indicated it was in the *READY* condition. He slid a switch one notch and the amber LEDs indicated *STANDBY—ENTER CODE TO RESTORE CONDITION TO READY.* Karl took a deep breath and sat beside Jill, who was utterly stunning in a burgundy suede business suit.

She rubbed his chronically tense *levator scapulae* muscle, from neck to shoulder blade. "I love to watch you sweat. What happens if it goes off?"

"You know very well, my masked maiden of mayhem. You're one of a very few people in the world who knows what it's for and where it is, or was."

"You don't think your old flame will spill the beans, do you?"

"Merely a precaution, new flame in the Bunsen burner of my cold, cold heart. She knows altogether too many details, names, places and dates, and no one can locate her, not even the Hip Hop boys. Those boys who are still alive, no thanks to Mr. Gubrious." Karl placed the failsafe device on a large red cushion, and reassembled the speakerphone.

"Your nerves are showing, Karl," said Jill as she removed her hand from his back. "Focus on the basics, it will help your anxiety. Are the uniforms ready?"

"Infected, bagged and ready for pickup and trucking early tomorrow morning, the day before Earth Day. I have the plant staff making some spares to keep them busy."

"Our munificent benefactors?"

"Safe as the innocent lambs in the fold for the next two weeks. You-know-who and the others will be at the elite armed forces competitive games in Iceland."

"So I hear. He likes me to call him 'Monty.' Do you know what he likes to call me?"

"I haven't the foggiest, pussy-cat of nine tails. I—"

The speakerphone rang with an organ tone. Jill stepped aside to be out of camera range. Karl rubbed his hands, appeared to put on a happy face, and pushed the button.

"Good morning. *Bonjour. Gutentag.*"

The screen faded in on Monty's imperial image. "Karl, old sport. Everything chippy chipper? Up, up and away?"

Karl absent-mindedly pounded the table for emphasis. "Yes, sir! Last three tests absolutely perfect! Bugs all ready to go!" Jill swiftly moved the red cushion and failsafe device from the path of Karl's fist.

"Spiffy! All systems go, and bugs away!" Monty pounded his table, with more force. "Karl, may I speak with her ladyship?"

"Who?!?"

"Her ladyship, the Duchess of Burgundy-Pimlico."

Jill oozed back into her chair, with a respectful nod to her royal benefactor. "Ever ready for you, Monty, darling."

"Tally-ho! Yacht's all ready to sail."

"I'm on my way. You are too, too kind, Monty dearest."

"Ta ta for now, saucy Wooster."

The screen faded to black and Karl hit the off button, looking at Jill in astonishment. "Your ladyship? Duchess of Burgundy-Pimlico? You did all that in one night?"

"All you said was that I should make him miss his speech and not hurt him. He's terribly lonely, and it just wouldn't do to allow someone of royal blood to marry a commoner, not to mention a penniless one." She flashed Karl a new diamond ring, picked up her dolphin skin attaché case and headed for the door.

"So after you're married you're positioned to inherit—"

"Most of his royal billions, not to mention his late wife's global mining and financial interests. Poor Ethne, so young, so tragic."

"Poor Monty, I should say. Is there any chance you will ease up on your kinky BDSM bedroom proclivities for His Royal Pecuniousness?"

"You think I should give up what *I* want just for someone else's benefit? *HA!* Now that is funny. *I* should change. *Ha-ha*. Wait 'til I tell Mr. Mucky-Pup."

She kissed Karl on the cheek and yanked his necktie tight, very tight.

"I can still keep you in my stable as my personal rodeo bull. Tally ho!" and she was off.

"Yes, your ladyship," said Karl with a theatrical bow.

Erik, Woody and Atlas were all showing a growth of beard and a considerable degree of dishevelment, and Erik had just enough voice left to finally bring his lecture to a conclusion. "So, if paying atten-tion you have been, you will now briefly sum-marize what you have learned, *dummkopf!*" Atlas stirred awake and whacked Woody on the knees with a fresh pointer, and finally pulled his sweat socks out of Woody's mouth.

"*Aaahh*, man, fresh air," said Woody, which earned him a whack on the back of the head. "OK, OK, what have we learned? We learned that the natural world is being destroyed by too many people, so we have to release a deadly bug, a very cleverly engineered bug, thanks to our brilliant Professor Pfizz, and to make the world safe for aristocracy all we have to do is kill about seven billion people."

Erik flew into a rage. "Only 6.8 billion! You must be ACCURATE! I will tolerate no errors and we will have 6.8 billion people eliminated *precisely*, no more, no less!! You, you, imbecilic, innumerate, Mr. Smelly Pants, *Vogel*-brain, you would exterminate 200 million people for the round off error? SO, you fail the test. No more of *der Palme schütteln* for you for the rest of your life! Now you will the surprise get."

Woody slipped into a dissociative state again, first picturing himself never experiencing the joy of wanking for the rest of his life, then reminding himself this might be no more than a few hours. His reverie was interrupted by a visitor.

Karl entered the study, gently holding the failsafe device on the red cushion.

"Karl! What do you think you are doing! The failsafe device!" said Erik.

Woody's eyes widened. "The *WHAT?!*"

Atlas gave Woody a sharp jab in the solar plexus with a tiny pile driver fist, knocking the wind out of him temporarily. "Your own filthy business you must mind, Mr. Stinky Boy."

Karl ignored the sideshow and addressed his mentor. "Merely a little precaution, just in case my previous paramount paramour pussycat loosens her tongue with the wrong people. Now where shall we, ah, the very place." Karl opened the bottom drawer of Erik's desk, eased the device and the cushion into place, covered it with several bags of Erik's marijuana stash, and closed the drawer slowly. "Mum's the word, everyone. You wouldn't tell anyone, would you Mr. Logan?"

Woody shook his head *No* with wrinkled lips shut.

"Good! Now if you will come with us, we will give you what you always wanted: we are going to make you a TV star."

Woody's eyes widened in terror as Karl, Erik and Atlas stared at him with fiendish little grins. Then the deadly silence was broken with a ripple of contagious snickers and chuckles, and finally escalated to a three part cacophony of booming maniacal laughter.

Tanya sat in the pilot's seat of the jet, balancing an ice pack on her head as she flew the small group over the Atlantic. Luciano briefly woke from his dozing in the co-pilot's seat, looked at her green complexion, shook his head and went back to sleep. In the rear seats, Lucia, Enrico and Mario munched buckets of deep fried chicken and grits.

Mei snuggled close to Lou in their seats just behind the cockpit. Lou completed a pencil sketch of Karl's lair in his notebook.

"So we could come in from the tunnel, but we're less likely to be caught if we go through the footpath in the forest, and in the back door. That's a bit longer but we should have enough time if we hustle. OK. Let's go over the failsafe device again."

Mei pointed to his sketch. "In the library, under the speaker phone. It can only be set off manually on the device itself or by Karl's cell phone."

"And the code to set it off is—"

"One last time, Lou. 2 1 4 2 5 8," she said rolling her eyes.

Lou scribbled the numbers into a small notebook. "214258, check. You're sure?"

"Yes I'm sure, for goodness sake. It's my birthday and Karl's, and I'll be right there if you forget. Lou, enough business talk, you're so serious." She gave her long black hair a seductive toss and hiked up her leather micro-mini skirt a notch. "So, tell, me, honestly, how do I look?"

"Fine, I guess. I don't pay much attention to clothes." Honestly meant honestly, didn't it?

"*Hmmm*, not much attention to clothes." She scanned his wrinkled, beige travel attire, speckled with coffee stains. "I'll bet you have a real passion for something exciting, Lou. Italian sports cars? Lamborghinis?"

"Lamborghinis! Now that is funny. Lamborghinis. Wait 'til I tell Tanya, *heh heh*, sports cars. No, I just have my good old 1957 Volkswagen Beetle."

"You're joking! A, a, a tiny *cheap* car, and an old one?"

"Sure! It's a classic, it still works like a charm and it gets great mileage. Frugality is a highly underrated virtue these days, and I'm very, very, frugal."

"F-Fru-! You just said that, that awful, horrible, word."

"Not just frugal, I might even go so far as to say parsimonious. You get that way when you live alone," said Lou.

"Alone! All alone, . . ." Mei fell into a hypnagogic state, a horrifying trance, a vision of the future so terrifying and shocking she could barely hold it in her conscious mind.

The violin strains of *None But the Lonely Heart* seemed to fill the cold air as she saw herself as a very old and frail woman, all alone in a shabby single room with one old mattress, peeling wallpaper and one 40 watt bulb for illumination. She shivered in her tattered clothes, torn woollen black stockings, and running shoes with holes. Her hair was grey and unkempt; her skin had suppurating sores brought on by malnutrition. With her few remaining yellowed and rotting teeth, she tried eating some cat food directly from the tin, using a plastic fork.

"Alone, alone and poor, forever . . ."

On this brilliantly sunny day in the French Alps, Atlas steered Woody's wheelchair down the mountain road, with Erik following closely behind on an electric scooter. They approached the main entrance of *The Mendel Research Laboratories*, where two Hip Hop boys slouched on guard.

Karl caught up with them on his four seater golf cart, with DeWang in the driver's seat. They wore the finest of casual golfing attire, with little logos of pneumonic plague bacteria on their golf shirts, designed by the Newfoundland fashion house of *Island of Lost Souls*.

"Woody, I hope you've enjoyed your last look at Mother Nature on this spectacularly gorgeous day!" said Karl with his usual sparkling smile. "Too bad it is your last day, but you did poke your nose into our little business on Kubrick Island, and you managed to incur the wrath of one of my sponsors."

"Now you want revenge, is that it?"

"Too harsh a word. Let's just call this your 'Comeuppance Day.' And just because you're such a curious fellow, like the proverbial cat, you get the grand tour. Gentlemen?"

The Hip Hop boys opened the double doors of the lab.

"We do have many visitors, usually much more illustrious than your ignoble self, Woody, and we like to start the tour with our agricultural research."

Karl led them inside the ground level floor of the lab, about two hectares in size. "Here we are testing new, all natural food crops, designed to maximize food yields, all done by selective breeding, and able to compete with any of the current genetically modified organisms. Upstairs we have projects in nano-technology to find more efficient ways to generate electricity from solar radiation, and to provide water in desert climates."

"Yeah, Karl, you're such a gentleman and a scholar," said Woody. "If you're going to kill me anyway, why don't you just shoot me now, you psychotic egomaniac?"

"Ah, the surly ingratitude of youth. Patience, Woody, please. The above ground part of the lab is for public show, so if you insist, we'll abbreviate the tour. This way, gentlemen."

Karl took them to a freight elevator and entered a six digit code. "The official visitors see no more than the labs above, and the storage area and loading docks one level down. We're going down considerably lower. Abandon all hope, Woody, for you enter here and do not come out." The elevator began to descend.

"Karl, I implore you," said Woody, "there is still time to stop. Everything you're doing, it's, it's just not right!"

"Right? Are you going all ethical on us at the last minute, Mr. Poke Your Nose In My Business? What's 'right' is what you can get away with."

With a jerk and a *clunk* they hit the lowest level, and Karl opened the waist high wooden elevator gates. The first thing that Woody saw was glass, thick gleaming glass walls from solid concrete floor to glass ceiling, reflecting and refracting the overhead and internal lighting in a blaze of technological splendour.

Atlas pushed Woody along a narrow service corridor which ran around the perimeter as far as he could see. They followed in a respectful last place, after Karl, Erik, and DeWang.

"Have your eyes adjusted yet, Woody?" said Karl. "Take a look at the centrepiece of our entire operation."

"Oh, my gosh! I suspected a duplicitous, evil, psychotic, genius such as Karl Mendel would have a secret, evil, laboratory hidden somewhere in his mountain lair, but I had no idea of the scale of your operation!"

"Why thank you, Woody. I'll take that as a compliment," beamed Karl. "Over here the last shipments of new uniforms for the Eco Angels have just arrived, and they go through an air-tight conveyor to the inside, where the entire internal staff must observe Level 4 Biohazard Protocols. Most of the work is automated, but sometimes nothing can do the job like good old human hands, right Professor?"

"*Ja,* especially for *sich einen von der Palme schütteln!"*

"Yes! Self gratification, precisely. Each uniform has an electronic tag which identifies the ultimate destination and volunteer. Over here, they are infected with a carefully calibrated dose of the appropriate level of pathogenicity. For some areas, the infections will last a few days and be effective for hundreds of thousands of deaths from one initial ever-loving hug from an Eco Angel."

Erik waved his reefer at Woody. "With the most advanced statistical methods, we have precisely calc-ulated the number of people to be eliminated at each location, including secondary and tertiary infec-tions as the fools run, panic and spread the disease even further. In some areas with the fewer volunteers and more excess humans to be eliminated, the single source can rid the planet of up to 2,718,281 surplus human individuals. In other areas, such as the agri-cultural communities where the selected elements of the population must be allowed to survive, we can limit the mortality to as few dead as we please."

"That invention of yours enables you to do all this so accurately? That telomere thing?" said Woody.

"The telomere-like molecular structure I have incorporated into the *Yersinia pestis* bacteria such precision allows, *ja.*"

"Woody, aren't you sorry you'll never get to tell the true story of Professor Erik Pfizz, the scientist saviour of the world?" said Karl.

"I'm sorry I couldn't get my mitts on your failsafe device, you psycho nut job."

"Manners, please, mind your manners, young man. Our penultimate stop is to the last automated station, where suits are sent through another conveyor with strict biohazard controls, sealed in airtight plastic, labelled, barcoded, and safely dropped onto a pallet for shipping."

Karl took a look at a sealed package from the pallet. "Wonderful, wonderful, wonderful. Have a look, Woody. This one is going to be worn by a Tammy Griffith, age 18, from Atlanta, Georgia. Tammy is going to celebrate Earth Day by going to a nearby seniors' housing project, The Golden Years Home for Retired Clansmen, with 811 residents, and hug every single Ku Klux Klan member she can find."

Woody strained as far as his bonds would allow him to get a look at the package. "For an insane egomaniac, Karl, I have to say your idea is not entirely bad."

"Now you're getting into the spirit of the game, Woody." Karl pulled out a green, non-toxic marker and wrote on the package: *Happy Earth Day, Tammy! Hugs, kisses and love, Karl. X O X O X.* "I just love sending people off into the wild blue yonder with a warm and fuzzy feeling in their hearts."

Karl pulled another plastic-wrapped suit from a different pallet. "Oh, my, young Francine Hatashita, 21, from Osaka, is our lucky winner today, Woody. She gets a dud."

"A dud?"

"Little Francine is going to celebrate Earth Day hugging all 1,286 scientists, engineers and technicians at the Osaka University Faculty of Bio-Medical Technology. We don't want to kill everyone, Woody, so she gets a clean suit. All hugs, no bugs. Let's just hope she doesn't stop off at the local prison or halfway house for a few extra hugs on the way home."

"So after you kill these billions of people, what happens next, Karl? Do you appoint yourself King of the World?"

"*King, hmmm,* great idea, but just a *li-ttle* pretentious, don't you think? But consider the possibilities, Woody. If I were drafted to take up such a position, despite my humble and self-effacing but feeble protests of unworthiness, I think 'President' might help to preserve the illusion of democracy. Perhaps 'Chairman,' if that's not too redolent of Mao, or 'Chancellor'—yes, I like that one. And then, after the big cleanup post Earth Day, perhaps I shall be cloned, thereafter simply be known as Karl the First, the first of a long line of Chancellors. Woody, you're very inspirational. I like you, I really like you!"

"Does this mean you're not going to kill me?"

"No."

They resumed their journey and soon arrived at the end of the corridor. DeWang poked his head behind a pair of large curtains, and stepped back with his hand on a rope. "All is ready, sir, precisely as specified."

"Now you get the surprise, Woody. I promised our benefactor a special end for the nosy Yankee newsman, and this is it. DeWang, if you please."

DeWang parted the curtains, revealing an acrylic glass cube, about three metres in each dimension, thick walled, with three banks of ceiling lights focussed on the centre. He then opened a solid acrylic glass door, rimmed with a black rubber seal on all sides.

"It is sad, Woody, that you won't be able to join us on our nice safe vacation in Iceland over the next few weeks. By then the plagues will have burned themselves out, there will be no evidence of anything other than a natural pandemic, and after a brief period of economic chaos and martial law, we will glide into the best of all possible worlds and live happily ever after." Karl gestured to the box, and Atlas rolled Woody inside.

"I thought you would like to be a TV star for your last appearance among the living. The camera to your left is connected to our internal cable system. And you will notice the black box to your right, with the vents pointing your way. When the red light on top starts flashing, you will have about one minute before the pathogens are released, and then infection is almost instantaneous. I hope you enjoy the show as much as we will. A healthy young man like you might even live for a few hours."

Atlas stepped out of the box and DeWang closed the door carefully, securing it with a large padlock. He clicked a wall switch and a large, steel door rose to an overhead niche, revealing a tunnel in the direction of the château.

"How much time do I have before then?"

"We're not going to tell you, Woody. It's going to be a surprise!"

"You're all completely nuts, crazier than a pack of three peckered owls at a barn dance!"

Woody struggled against his bonds as Karl, Atlas and DeWang stepped into the golf cart.

Karl lifted his hands like a conductor, and said, "Gentlemen, a friendly send-off for Mr. Logan. And-a one, and-a two, and-a three!" Karl, Atlas and DeWang broke into song, while Erik merely moved his lips.

"Happy trails, dear Woody, we may never meet again, . . ."

Lou babbled on, oblivious to the internal world of his new companion. "So, you could say it is truly possible for two different realities to exist at the same time! Can you believe that? And that's the story of Schrödinger's cat. Isn't quantum mechanics truly wonderful? Mei?"

Mei opened one eye, murmured a little *mmm-Hmm*, and went back to sleep.

"But on a macroscopic level, the real fun is in trying to understand complex dynamic systems, which, as I'm sure you know, are inherently unstable and unpredictable; they're extremely sensitive to very small changes in their initial conditions. It's like the butterfly effect, everyone knows that one, in which the minute atmospheric disturbance caused by a butterly flapping its wings in Beijing could conceivably start a chain reaction of changes that might eventually affect an entire weather system in Florida, maybe even help create a hurricane. The fate of the world could hinge on one tiny, apparently inconsequential, thing that changes slightly and no one even notices. Gosh, that's an exciting concept, isn't it?"

Lou looked about the plane for a response. Mei was out cold, her mouth open wide enough for Lou to admire the gold filling on her lower left wisdom tooth. Tanya was dozing in the cockpit with one bloodshot eye on the autopilot. His family were all sound asleep after their latest feeding. So, no one but Lou noticed one small, rather dull looking butterfly which must have come aboard before takeoff, and was now flapping its tiny wings, first in one direction, and then the other.

CHAPTER 12

Is this how the world as we know it comes to an end?

On a brilliant full moon night on a footpath through an alpine forest, Tanya and Mei waited impatiently for Lou, who was a few metres away behind a copse of bushy pines, attending to nature's call. Tanya, like Lou, was dressed in night camouflage gear and camouflage makeup. Mei had reluctantly acquiesced to the need for non-reflective clothing, and sported a designer black suede jumpsuit and black suede boots.

"Lou, I do not believe this! In few hours, most of humanity will be destroyed by madman and you have to make wee-wee time. Shake a leg! Sorry, I mean please to hurry."

Well out of sight, Lou was hunched over to hide his new digital device, whatever these new fangled things were called now, with both thumbs working furiously to send a text message. In the bright moonlight he could easily read the hastily scribbled numbers on his notepad, entered six digits and pressed *send*. "I can't help it, nature makes me nervous."

Mei just rolled her eyes and paced about, muttering "Men! *Oh!*"

Lou finally emerged and offered a shrug and a "Sorry. I feel much better now."

"That makes us all very happy, you feeling better," said Tanya. "Now we have need for speed."

Another few hundred metres and the forest trail ended at an open field. Lou took the night vision binoculars from Tanya and surveyed the scene. About 100 metres away was a tall chain link fence topped with razor wire, surrounding the gardens and smaller buildings near the château. An army style barracks lay further downhill, midway between the château and the laboratory. "There's a small group of Hip Hop boys near the barracks, smoking and drinking. One sitting on a chair near the front of the château looks like he's asleep. No one near the back door."

"Is so far exactly as promised, Mei," said Tanya.

"If they haven't changed the codes, we're in. You won't hurt Karl, will you? Please, please, Lou?" said Mei.

"Like I promised, no killing unless absolutely necessary. All we need to do is to get to the library, find the failsafe device and blow the lab. Then we're done."

Mei nodded and led them in silence to the gate nearest the château.

Karl sat in his comfy lecture hall chair in Erik's study, using the remote control to click through endless channel choices. He chose the *Closed Circuit* menu and flipped through on-line images of the labs, the château exterior, the parking lot, and finally settled on the image of Woody tied to his chair in the glass booth, struggling hopelessly. Erik and Atlas broke into a short round of polite applause.

"A tribute to your genius, Professor, this sacrificial lamb." said Karl. "That young man should adopt the attitude of the Roman gladiators, who would say to the Emperor, *Hail Caesar, those who are about to die salute you."*

Atlas stood at attention and clicked his heels. "Whole world must be salute Professor Pfizz, Doktor Mendel, saving they be, all life on planet." He thrust his right hand up at a 45° angle. Erik wagged a finger and whispered, *"Nein, nein,* the other one." Atlas morphed his salute to the Allies' version and touched his fingertips to his eyebrow.

"You are too generous," said Erik, returning his subordinate's salute, "I have merely tinkered with some of the nature's little secrets; it is Karl who the lion's share of the credit is deserving."

The mutual admirations were interrupted by DeWang, who came into the study bearing a large platter with four bowls of plain popcorn.

"We apologize for the paucity of the late night snacks, gentlemen. If you wish, we can still prepare a more substantial dinner. A roasted bird, with a novel stuffing, or perhaps a barbecued Civet cat? Jamaican style jerk Siamese kittens?"

Karl protested, "This will do admirably, DeWang, come and join us. It's not the first time we have had to skip a few meals preparing for the big day. The big banquet will have to keep for a few days. Let's settle back and watch Mr. Logan's finest hour, shall we?"

The onscreen image of Woody continued to struggle with his restraints. He tried biting the plastic handcuffs, and the audience broke into applause, cheers, and derisive laughter.

At the edge of the forest, Luciano, Enrico and Mario watched as Lucia followed Lou's group through her night vision binoculars. "She's puttin' some numbers in. I think she's goin' a 1, 7, 2, 9, and it's open!"

"So far, she's a-tellin' the truth," said Luciano, "but I still gotta my doubts."

"Good, she's got it open, she lets Tanya go in the gate first, then Lou, then—hey, wait a minute! She goes and puts in some extra numbers while the other guys weren't even lookin' at her. *Puttana!*" said Lucia, keeping her eyes on Mei.

"She's up-a to no good, that *goomah*!" said Luciano. "What about-a the layout?"

Lucia whispered, "Two trucks between the long skinny house and the big house." "*Eccellente!*" said Luciano. "We gonna make-a the stand there, and draw their fire away from-a Luigi." He clapped his twin boys on the shoulders.

"Those hippin' and-a hoppin' boys gonna get-a the big surprise."

A large, male figure silently crept behind the thick bushes near the lab entrance, and checked his text messages one last time. He carried a crossbow, quiver, an automatic pistol, and wore a camouflage Kevlar vest equipped with a climbing rope, six throwing knives, and one gigantic Bowie knife in a back sheath. As he watched, two Hip Hop boys emerged from the building, pistols stuck in the rear of their baggy shorts.

The first pulled out a package of smokes, lit a cigarette, and offered one to his partner. He would have made the offer verbally, but before the words could come out of his throat, a crossbow bolt went in and pinned his larynx to the doorframe. A second bolt hit his partner in precisely the same spot, and he quietly crumpled in a heap, face down.

The dark figure quietly removed the cigarette from the mouth of the late Mr. Chen, stomped it out on the ground, took the key chain from his belt, and disappeared into the darkened laboratory.

Somewhere far down the mountain road, a caravan of tractor trailers headed toward Mendel Laboratories with engines straining. Each truck had an identical sign: *FPS Express—anywhere on earth in 24 hours or it's free.*

DeWang brought four more bowls of fresh popcorn into Erik's study. All eyes were on Woody's energetic farewell performance, which helped to keep his audience awake and alert despite the long wait. The more he struggled with the duct tape holding him to the chair, or scraped his wrists trying to free himself from the plastic handcuffs, the more sadistic laughter came from the audience. Woody finally gave up the struggle, broke down and started crying with great heaving sobs. Atlas burst into a wolf-like howl and began rolling about on his mat, laughing like a hyena.

A flashing red message, *Security Alert*, was superimposed on the grainy black and white image of Woody. Karl pushed a few buttons on the remote and the image of three figures appeared, approaching the château by the rear entrance.

"Mei, bless you, and bless your compulsive loyalty." He pulled a small pistol from his jacket and gestured to DeWang. As they left he said, "Enjoy the show Professor, Atlas. I may have to watch it on the videodisk version."

Woody sat slumped in his chair, sobbing, as a gentle knock on the glass door roused him. "Who the—hey, wait a minute, I know you! You're that Egyptian boxer, Joe Falooka!"

"And who are you, sir?"

"Woody Logan, ECO TV News."

"May I ask what you're doing in there?" said Joe, fumbling with the key chain.

"I'm about to be poisoned by a lunatic and his horrible pet bacteria. Just get me out of here. Open the bloody door, damn it!"

"Don't swear, it's not nice!" Joe tried one key after another.

"Don't leave me here!"

"Sorry, I can't get it open."

"When that red light starts flashing, there are going to be about a billion germs let loose in here. Hurry up, for God's sake!"

"I said don't swear! No blasphemy!" Joe slammed the box with his fist, shaking the door on its hinges.

"Hey, I remember your story now. I used to cover sports in college. You went berserk in the ring when some guy was swearing and you almost killed him! You can't stand foul language. Joe Falooka. Well, Jesus H. 'Hop-along' Christ on a pogo stick."

Joe pounded the booth with both fists, and the hinges loosened a fraction of an inch. "Stop that! Stop it now!"

"It moved! The door moved! You almost got it, big guy. OK, now hear this!"

Erik and Atlas sat eating popcorn, watching the big show. Erik looked at his watch. "Any second now. We will the pathogen spray see, then he will start the coughing."

"Professor, microphone we be need, he seem be saying something. And now picture shaking. Hard tell what he say is."

Erik leaned closer to the screen. "I think he something about his *mother* said. Now *forget you, mother freak* or something like that, *can't, smell he can't, can't face, shed head* maybe, then *Gott a mitt*. No sense he is making. Wait—I think now he is trying to seek *succour. Jaaah*, he must be praying!"

The red light on the box started to flash as Joe tried a flying drop-kick, and the door finally popped off its hinges.

"Sorry, sorry sir, I apologize for my language, I'm very sorry. Would you mind switching those things off? Please?"

"It's a good thing you said you're sorry." Joe turned off the black box and the TV camera, and quickly slashed Woody's bonds with his Bowie knife. "Let's get out of here; I've got to blow this place up."

"Yeah, and you want the failsafe device, right?"

"How did you know about that?"

"I know where it is—they moved it! Come on, I'll show you."

Woody and Joe raced up the tunnel to the château.

Luciano, Enrico, Mario and Lucia hid behind the two trucks between the château and the Hip Hop barracks. They were in a prime position to defend against an attack from the barracks or a rear assault from the château.

"Papa, how much time?" whispered Mario, shivering as the morning sun began to creep over the mountains.

"Just a few minutes," said Luciano, checking his watch. "Lou said timing gotta be perfect."

Mei led Lou and Tanya through the darkened kitchen and storage areas in the basement, finally to a sturdy door with a digital combination lock. She punched in a code and whispered, "Not even Karl uses this passage anymore. We'll be safe if we're quiet." Lou followed her, one hand on a dusty railing, the other in his pocket, quietly sending a text message. Tanya held her pistol at the ready.

She closed the door behind her, making no more noise than a baby mouse urinating on a soft blotter.

A flight of centuries old stone steps later, they paused at a landing, facing a modern steel door which seemed out of place in the ancient passageway. Mei said, "The steps go all the way up to the roof, past the master bedroom. This is the door we want. After I open this door, absolute silence while we go through the chapel, then the library is practically across the hall. There should be no one on this floor at this hour."

Tanya nodded. Lou stifled a sneeze, then nodded. Mei looked through a peephole, slowly turned a brass knob and opened the door, emerging into the chapel through a wooden panel between the organ and the grandfather clock. There was just enough sunlight now peeking over the mountains to outline a few features of the chapel.

Mei walked on cat feet past three stone pillars, turned and held up a palm. Tanya and Lou froze beside the middle pillar. Mei slid around the hallway door, leaving only her palm in sight.

Tanya would have looked to Lou for reassurance, but she thought the better of it when the steel muzzle of a pistol pressed into her neck.

"Kindly refrain from any manner of motion, if you please, madam," said DeWang, emerging from the shadow behind the pillar and taking the pistol from Tanya's now relaxed grip.

Mei stepped back into the room, and turned on the lights. Karl stepped out from behind the grandfather clock, a pearl and silver pistol pointed at Lou.

"Luigi Gubriace," said Karl with mannered menace.

"Call me Lou, please."

Mei rushed over to Karl and glued herself to his ribs.

DeWang finished a quick pat down of Tanya and Lou, and said, "We have confiscated merely one pistol and two cell phones. No other weapons were to be found, sir."

"Lou, Lou, you came all this way and you forgot to pack a gun?"

"I think I left it in Mei's hotel room. Beside the bed. Loaded. We had other things on our minds. Sorry."

"And you, my one and only main squeeze, you came back to me." Karl gave Mei a hug, and added, "When I see you, O bona fide bird of paradise, my heart bursts forth with joy and soars through the sky like a great eagle."

Lou whispered to Tanya, "Can you believe she actually swallows that romantic gobbledygook?"

Tanya whispered to Lou, "Hook, line and stinker."

Mei's talons dug inextricably into Karl's ribcage. "I can forgive your indiscretions and infidelities, Karl, but *he* has unforgivably bad taste, absolutely no class. Look at those cheap, shabby clothes, the dirty shoes, that awful haircut. So common and working class it's disgusting. And listen, this will kill you Karl, do you know what he drives? An old, dirty, cheap, proletarian *Volkswagen! Hah!* And do you know what he said to me, immaculately groomed and impeccably perfectly mannered Karl? He actually said the *F*-word to me!"

"*F*-word?"

Mei stuck her tongue out at Lou and Tanya rolled her eyes. "Frugal. *Da*. Now I get flip-flop."

Luciano kept his eyes on his watch as he counted down from five with his fingers, watching the first of the Hip Hop boys emerge from the barracks into the early morning sun. "NOW!" he shouted, and Enrico and Mario launched rocket propelled grenades at the barracks.

"Here they come!" Enrico relished a good fight, and he was about to get one from the hordes of Hip Hop boys rushing from the burning building. Mario always liked to keep things interesting with a small side bet. "Ten bucks for each one we hit, bro'?"

Luciano found time to smack him on the ear. "Hey, you mugs, no needless killing. Just keep them busy and pinned down for a few minutes, until, you know?"

The sounds of automatic gunfire and grenades bursting resonated throughout the chapel. Karl looked up in surprise.

"Don't worry, sweetie, that's their excuse for a backup plan. And there's only four of them." Mei blew Lou an uncharacteristically vulgar Bronx cheer.

"Our boys can handle them," said Karl.

Mei hissed, "*His* team are all Italian. And they're all fat. Fat, fat, fat! Like her."

In a momentary lapse in confidence, Tanya looked at her own trim, athletic figure. Karl and DeWang gave her the once-over. Karl threw Lou a *Not bad, eh?* look, and Lou responded with a *How should I know?* shrug.

Erik and Atlas sat in the study, munching popcorn, staring at a blank screen.

"*Awww!* Always happen, Professor, picture out go just before best part," said Atlas.

Before Erik could respond, the interior door of the study sprang open, and Joe flew into the room, pistol ready, followed by Woody.

Atlas made a move to get up and Joe aimed at the pupil of his nearest eye. "Don't even think about it," said Joe.

Woody picked up three wooden pointers from a quiver behind the desk. He cracked the first one over Atlas' head. A blink and silent grimace from Atlas. "Sit down, squirt." The second shattered on his kneecap, eliciting an involuntary *Ooooh!* "Shut up, twerp." The third broke on his nose with a secondary crack as the tiny nose bone fractured. *Aaaargh!* "And don't even think about using any curse words!"

Joe rolled his eyes. "Woody? Time to save the world? Remember?"

Woody went straight to the desk drawer and removed the failsafe device from Erik's stash, the red *READY* light flashing. Woody poised his index finger over the keypad, and looked to Joe.

Joe kept his aim on Atlas and Erik, glanced at his watch and said, "Time's up on your evil plan, Professor. Woody, if you please, in 10, 9, 8, . . ."

Karl took aim at Lou's chest. "It pains me to say it, but you know I have to kill you now, Lou. We could have had some great conversations, but, alas, time is running out."

Lou nodded and said, "I understand, completely. But before you do, may I ask you just one question? Just a few seconds, I promise."

"All right, but no speeches! No pleading for mercy, no debates about how to save the world."

"Of course not, it's far too late for that," said Lou, drawing his words out slowly. "You're a very busy man, you have things to do, places to be, billions to kill, and I have too much respect for your time. So, here's my question." Lou took a slow breath and pointed to the grandfather clock.

"Is that clock accurate?"

"Huh?!?" said Karl.

All eyes turned to the grandfather clock. The hands clicked over to 6:00 AM and it began to chime the hour.

The explosion was so powerful the people in the chapel felt the building rock and watched dust shake loose from all sides, before their brains could begin to process the loudest sound they had ever heard in their lives. Lou grabbed Tanya's hand and dove behind a pillar, away from the line of fire of the menacing pistols.

Mei's heart shattered into a million tiny slivers as Karl jumped into the secret passage by the organ and slammed the door behind him. A fractured heartbeat later, a hand reached out from the hidden passage and pulled Mei inside, slamming the door and ramming the bolt home with a loud *clunk*.

Woody and Joe flew into the chapel, and with one look at Joe, DeWang dropped his pistol and Tanya's and held his hands up high over his head. Curiously, his polished accent and manners dropped too. "Peace, dawg."

Tanya rushed to snatch her pistol and tried to re-open Karl's bolt hole.

"And don't waste your time, bi—lady, no way that thing's gonna open," said DeWang.

"We got to get him!" said Tanya, pounding on the door with her pistol.

"Forget that dude, the second failsafe's gonna go! He got to destroy all his records and computers here too. After the lab blows this place is wired to blow in minutes. Dang it, humongous homie, we gotta run *NOW!*"

"Good enough for me. We're done here," said Lou, and he led Joe, Woody, Tanya and DeWang in a race through the château and down the mountain road.

Woody jogged alongside Lou. "Any comments for ECO TV News *now*, Mr. Gubriace?"

"Off the record, some days I wonder if humanity is worth saving."

Karl and Mei emerged from the ancient passage to the highest turret of the château. Karl untied and yanked back the camouflaged canvas sheet, revealing a large hang glider. He quickly checked a few critical points, and pulled the glider's harness onto his back.

"This is built for a single passenger, my lithe and lovely one. You will have to cling on to me. Can you handle that?

"Cling? *Moi?* You just watch me cling!" Mei hugged Karl around the waist as he snapped the last harness clips into position. He stepped up to the edge of the parapet, knelt on one knee and offered a hand to assist his lady fair onto his back. "Have a whiff of the fresh, neutral breeze from Switzerland. A few hundred metres in the air, over the next peak, and then it's literally a walk in the park to safety, aerodynamic angel of my airwaves."

"Karl, you're always the consummate gentleman, you have such style, such passionate, romantic eloquence, and above all, you have such perfect manners. But dearest, do you, can you, ever really, truly, love me?"

"Love is an illusion, a delicious bit of evolutionary prestidigitation, a hormonal *legerdemain*, Mother Nature's psycho-biological scam to perpetuate our selfish genes, and we believe in it merely because we are programmed to believe in it, O deliciously divine diva of my delusionary dreams. When love fails, as all illusions must fail, manners must suffice."

They leapt off the turret into the morning wind and the glider sailed serenely into the mountain sunrise.

The following day, the floor director of the ECO TV studio in Paris counted down from five and gave the *go* cue.

"Good evening, everyone, and a Happy Earth Day to all eight billion of us and to every living being on our Mother Earth. This is Neville Lear sitting in for Woody Logan. On tonight's special Earth Day show—"

Woody rushed onto the set, still wearing the same stinky clothes and with several days' growth of beard. He roughly pushed Neville's chair off to the side and stared directly into the camera, with a sleep deprived, red-eye glare.

"It's all a conspiracy! They tried to kill us, billions of us dead! The rich and powerful are trying to take over the world."

Lamont and Cranston rushed onstage and took an arm each.

Woody continued, now raving, "It was Karl Mendel behind all the plagues, he did it! He's insane! They're all raving, mad, balmy, nuts, cuckoo, crackers, completely round the bend, loony-toony!"

Cranston spoke quietly but firmly. "It's game over, Mr. Logan. Done. *Finito*. Concluded. Final curtain. End of story."

"He'll be back! He'll be back, just you wait and see! You haven't heard the last of this conspiracy. There's got to be a sequel!" shouted Woody on his way to a far, far better rest than he had ever known.

Neville, ever the consummate professional, regained his position on the set and quietly addressed the audience. "I must apologize for that outburst, ladies and gentlemen. An utterly ludicrous story, and raving about a conspiracy is a sure sign of a troubled mind. Karl Mendel conspiring to—*heh, heh, heh*—the notion would be laughable if it were not so sad. Ours is a very stressful profession at times, and Mr. Logan appears to have been under considerable personal and professional strain. Perhaps we might arrange for some psychiatric treatment for Mr. Logan in North Korea, or possibly at a well known Russian psychiatric institute, where some experimental drugs might relieve him of certain psychotic delusions, or perhaps he might be given a lobotomy performed by an inebriate intern with a hacksaw, or—I must apologize for my digression, and for the unseemly behaviour of an uncouth former colleague. I would like to reassure our viewers that he will be taken care of, very, very, well taken care of, indeed."

"Some sad news for the Mendel Foundation. An early morning fire broke out at the Mendel Laboratories yesterday, and spread to Dr. Mendel's home in the French Alps. Authorities suspect that a terrorist group may be responsible, possibly the anti-environmental and pro-capitalist terrorist organization, *Let the Eagle Soar for Freedom*. Fortunately, the local ECO TV news service was able to catch it all on helicopter video."

A video insert showed the fire still blazing and the survivors rushing down the mountain road. A large group of Hip Hop boys *pimp rolled* down the mountain as fast as their low crotch pants would allow. Lou's team followed behind, and in the rear were Erik in his wheelchair with Atlas trotting beside him. In the distance, a barely visible hang glider crossed the nearest peak.

"Fortunately, at the time of the fire Dr. Mendel was in Iceland, a guest of—ah, yes, we have that video now."

A second video insert showed an elegant garden party, with a string quartet playing *An English Country Garden*. DeWang served champagne, and Erik and Atlas munched on popcorn off in a corner by themselves. Karl, Mei, Monty and Jill appeared to be holding a polite conversation, as Monty guffawed loudly.

"There is Dr. Mendel now, with his beautiful fiancée. I apologize for the audio quality, but I think Dr. Mendel is saying, 'OK, but next time, no more Mr. Nice Guy.' *Hmmmph?* Very curious statement. And the host, yes, there he is, His Royal Highness, as he likes to be called, Prince Montgomery of Saxe-Coburg and Gotha. With him is his new bride, the Duchess of Burgundy-Pimlico, Dr. Jillian Fleming. Very lovely, indeed. Something of a whirlwind romance, I am told."

Neville came back on camera and said, "All over the world, people are holding Earth Day parties. Our roving reporter in North America, Sapphira Jones, has joined a typical celebration in progress."

Sapphira touched her earpiece, and picked up the cue. "Thank you, Neville. I hope you can hear me over the music. These people are loving every minute of Earth Day and boy do they know how to party—just look at them go!" An accordion quartet and percussionist played and sang *Tomorrow, tomorrow, why do today what you can put off until tomorrow!* as Lou and Tanya, Joe and Lucia, and Luciano and Magda all danced, in their own fashion, while Enrico and Mario grappled each other in a sumo match.

"And finally, it's sad to have to report that our poor old Mother Earth is not doing at all well. The latest statistics indicate further increases in temperatures across the globe, severe water shortages in East Africa and South Asia, continued armed conflicts and innumerable dead around the world. Today's tally of species loss is oceanic 14, tropical regions 12, temperate regions 9, and polar regions no score. But, let's forget all about the bad news, and just have a great party and celebrate Earth Day! Enjoy yourselves, and remember what my grandmother, Granny Lear, used to say: *Never fear, never worry, Mother Nature will always find a way to save the day.*"

CHAPTER 12 ½

OR is this how the world as we know it comes to an end?

The Butterfly Effect

A cloud passed over the moon, diminishing the available light to nearly zero. Tanya and Mei were barely visible to each other, only a few feet apart on a narrow mountain trail, while Lou was behind some bushy pines answering the call of nature. Lou and Tanya's night camouflage gear and makeup were superfluous in the darkness, and only occasionally did Mei's highly polished black latex jumpsuit and dark python skin boots pick up a twinkle of starlight.

Tanya spoke in a loud whisper. "Lou, you choose worst possible time for everything. Can we please save billions of peoples first, then Lou can pass water at leisure. Please Lou, just take a leak and get it over with, *da?*"

From the other side of the bush, Lou shielded the dim light of his new digital device with his jacket, and tried in vain to read the numbers scribbled into his notebook. "Sorry, when I get out here in the dark, with bugs and snakes all around, all my innards just seize up. Can I help it if I'm a city person and not an outdoorsman? I'm getting close to an anxiety attack."

"Just think about Niagara Falls, car washes, water cannons hosing down crowds of filthy rabble; go with the flow, will you?" said Mei.

"Not helping."

"Lou, is trouble with number one or number two?" said Tanya.

"Both, now that I think—*Hey!*—that's a bit better. It helps if I can get my mind off my bladder and think about something else, like numbers, ciphers or something. Tanya, what's the entry code for your condo?"

"Lord love a duck! Code is my birthday, 1411." said Tanya.

"1, 4, 1, 1. Almost there, almost. *Fiddlesticks!* Mei, the code, that was 214259, wasn't it?"

"No, 214258. Got it?"

"Got it, 2, 1, 4, 2, 5, 8, thanks," said Lou, and he entered the six numbers and pressed *send*. "Oh yes, it worked. *Aaaaaaahhhhhhh*, relief. Yessssss."

A moment later, Lou returned to the trail and said, "That's much better. Thanks for the distraction."

"How could you forget something so vital? It's just the digits of my birthday and Karl's."

"I must have mixed it up with someone else's birthday, maybe Jill's." As soon as the J-word was out of his mouth, Lou wished he could take it back. "Sorry, sorry, it just slipped out."

Mei froze for a second, and said, "OK, I'll be OK. I'll try to deal with this in a mature way, without bursting into tears or getting angry. I am a mature woman with complete control of my faculties. I know the alpha male of my dreams has dumped me for a cheap, kinky, slut, but that is no reason to be *emotional!*" She took a few deep breaths, blinked away a little tear, smiled a stoic smile, and gave Lou's shoulder a squeeze. "Thank you, Lou, for reminding me of why we're really here."

"And that would be?" said Lou.

"We're here to show that loathsome lothario, that licentious libertine, that self-serving, scum sucking, *SWINE* Karl that he can't fool around behind my back and get away with it!"

"And—?" said Lou, gesturing for more.

"And to save the world; after I deal with Karl." She reached into her designer handbag and pulled out a small 9 mm pistol, her hand shaking. "I want the first shot at Karl, and I will shoot him right in the ego."

Lou recognized the pistol he must have left in Mei's hotel room. "I think I should take that for now." He gently removed the pistol from her shaking hand, which offered no resistance.

Tanya said, "We must go now, have some distance to travel, and sun will be up before too long."

Further down the path, Tanya looked ahead with her night vision binoculars. "Lou, is open field ahead, must be more careful."

Mei borrowed the binoculars and surveyed the scene. "There's a high fence surrounding the perimeter, and the gate I told you about is 100 metres ahead. No guards at the back of the house or near our path. There's one guard at the front of the house, sound asleep in a chair. I think it's Mr. Cho. He always nods off on night shift. There's one light on in the professor's study, but that's normal. He usually dozes off, watching animal porn films of fornicating sheep and wanking himself silly."

Lou looked at Tanya and shook his head.

Mei continued. "Everyone else in the house should have fallen asleep hours ago. There's another bunch of Hip Hop boys near the barracks, about 200 metres down the road to the lab. I know those guys: they smoke, drink and play poker for pennies all night long. The rest of them, the day shift, are probably in the barracks trying to sleep while the party animals are making too much noise. Some bodyguards. We should be just fine if we are completely quiet."

Lou took the binoculars for a second opinion. "It all looks exactly as described. So far, so good, Mei."

"Will you let me deal with Karl? I want him to suffer for what he did."

"After the lab is blown up, you can have Karl and do whatever you want. Ram him full of garlic bread stuffing and roast him on a spit for an Earth Day dinner if that's what would make you feel justice has been served."

"*Bon appetit*," said Tanya. "Let's get crackink."

Mei stifled a giggle and led them to the gate in the fence.

Karl sat in his favourite reclining chair in Erik's study, cleaning his teeth with a toothpick in one hand, flipping through channels with a TV remote control with the other. He finally settled on the image of Woody in the glass booth. Erik was nodding off in his chair, and Atlas yawned a mighty yawn for his size.

DeWang entered, pushing a food cart laden with fine crystal bowls. "For the big show tonight, gentlemen, we have your choice of plain buttered popcorn, Texas barbecue flavoured popcorn, old cheddar and seven hot chilli pepper popcorn, white chocolate sauce over broccoli popcorn, smoked sea snake and oyster popcorn, bacon and egg popcorn, maple syrup poutine popcorn, SPAM-oil roasted popcorn, tofu popcorn simulate, cinnamon and chipotle popcorn, and Professor Pfizz's favourite, blue popping corn popped in oil of hashish."

Karl looked up at his trusted gentleman's gentleman. "DeWang, you are too kind, but I could not eat another bite. My compliments to you for a marvellous dinner, the last big feast before the big day. The bird was utterly delectable, such a unique flavour, but I can't quite place it. Bald eagle? Whooping crane?"

DeWang allowed himself a rare feeling of pride, betrayed by a tiny smile. "Not this time, Dr. Mendel, we thought something more rare would be suitable as a prelude to the upcoming festivities on Earth Day. California condor."

"Condor! Wonderful, DeWang, wonderful, it's been months since we last enjoyed one. It usually has a strong and gamey flavour, but the koala stuffing and fresh mint sauce went so well with the condor."

"*Ja*, and the fine Rhine valley wines, schnapps, strudel, cheesecakes, such a banquet. I could all night and all day sleep."

"Thank you, gentlemen, we are honoured."

"Let's settle back and watch *The Woody Logan Show*, the final episode in which our hero shows us how a not so macho young man dies," said Karl.

Erik stared at Woody's image, and said, "I wish that static *Drecksack* would do something interesting. He just sits there, waiting for the end."

Karl yawned a great yawn. "We ought to have invested in a top quality, high definition camera, or two cameras, with a decent microphone. Then we could have added some proper lighting, maybe some music for Mr. Logan's last hours. This could have been part of a great documentary for posterity. As it stands, it's so boring I'm having trouble keeping awake so far." *Yawn.*

The yawn contagion spread from Karl, to DeWang, to Atlas, and to Erik, who said, "It is good thing I can without the sleep for days go. But now I just my eyes close, only for a few seconds, *mmm.*"

At the end of the forest trail, Luciano shook his head. "I'm-a no trustin' that little rich girl. Hey, Lucia, what's she doin'?" Enrico and Mario stared toward Lou's group, barely visible in the gloomy pre-dawn night.

Lucia focussed her binoculars at the gate in the security fence. "Lou, move your butt to the left, just a few inches, YES! I can see her now. She goes a 1, 7, 2, 9 and, and, it's open. All right! Just like she said."

"So far, she's a-tellin' the truth," said Luciano, "but I still gotta my doubts."

"OK, the gate's open, Tanya goes in first, Lou is second, and hey—what's the skinny little bee-yotch up to—she's lookin' around, lookin' at the château, lookin' at the number pad, looks back to Lou. Now she's leavin' the gate open a bit, yeah, just like she said!" said Lucia.

"Maybe she's-a OK, that *goomah*," said Luciano.

"Papa, it's so cold!" bellowed Enrico, rubbing his hands together.

Luciano smacked him on the head. "Quiet, you big, dumb ox!" he whispered. "Those hippin' and-a hoppin' boys aren't deaf! You wanna spoil Luigi's big-a plan?" He smacked Mario on the head too, and added, "And-a you, don't even think about makin' a noise."

Lucia whispered, "Shhh, quiet you guys. Look, it's still totally dark, so like we can get to them two trucks between the little house and the big house. We can make a big noise and draw everyone's attention."

"Those hippin' and-a hoppin' boys ain't gonna know what's-a hittin' them."

Mr. Chen stood under the door light at the lab entrance, and Mr. Chan stood a few feet off, away from the light's glare, as they enjoyed their smoke break, shivering in the cold night, paying no attention to the slight rustle of the large bushes nearby.

"We should stop this unhygienic, antisocial, and carcinogenic activity, Mr. Chen. Perhaps we shall cease and desist from smoking; shall we say right after Earth Day?"

"I find it impossible to kick the habit, Mr. Chan, I just love to smoke, and smoke, and smoke some more. I live to smoke, the ritual of lighting up, the creation of tension with a few minutes of abstinence, the orgasmic release with the first inhalation, so much better than sex, and lasts longer, too. I could chain smoke these American cigarettes all day and all night. Nothing could make me stop smoking. I would rather die than qui—"

A crossbow bolt punctuated Mr. Chen's last words and pinned his neck to the doorframe. A second bolt might have hit his partner squarely in the larynx as well, but in the dim light the shot went low, into his heart. He had just enough life energy to struggle with the bolt, stagger a few paces, and say "Gosh, darn it!" before he quietly tumbled onto the ground and rolled onto his back.

A large, dark figure emerged from the bushes and quietly kicked the cigarette from the mouth of the late Mr. Chen, and took the key chain from his belt. He saw a second key chain on the sprawled figure on the ground and took that too before melting into the blackness of the laboratory.

A few kilometres down the mountain road, the captain of a caravan of tractor trailers picked up the company cell phone. "Good morning, FPS Express—anywhere on earth in 24 hours or it's free." His driver pretended not to be listening. "No sir, in fact the traffic is light and the road is in good shape. We should get there on time or even early."

DeWang awoke with a snort and stood at attention, still half in dream land. "More popcorn, sir? A few sandwiches? A small snifter of absinthe, cognac, or cointreau to aid the digestion? After dinner mints? Nuts?"

Karl rolled his eyes open and wrapped his blanket tighter. "Relax, DeWang, relax, you've done more than enough with that marvellous dinner." He looked at Erik, sound asleep, gripping a lamb fleece comforter on his lap.

Karl closed his eyes again and said, "Atlas, what's he doing now?"

Atlas rolled over on his mat, near Erik's chair. "Just sit there still he be, with eye close, mutter same thing many time."

"Can you make it out?" murmured Karl.

"Think it be prayer or mantra. We watch man meditate." Atlas curled up on his mat again.

As Karl slipped into sleep he said, "Yes, Mei dear. Turn the TV off, please."

Soon the only sounds in the study were a few light snores, the occasional whoosh or squeak or *pop!* of breaking wind, and the odd tummy rumble, perhaps an acoustical gesture of protest from one of the last California condors on earth.

Woody sat erect in his chair, softly chanting a sacred mantra, overheard long ago at a weekend workshop on sexual tantric yoga for success.

"Om mani padme dum-de-dum. Om mani padme dum-de-dum."

An enormous male figure stood by the glass door, knocking gently. "Sir? Sir? Sorry to disturb you, but who are you and what on earth are you doing in there?"

Woody's quiet meditation may have helped still his nerves; he decided to open his eyes only slightly, moving his lips gently. "I'm Woody Logan, ECO TV News team, and there are several psychotic lunatics watching me on closed circuit TV right now. I can't quite see you, sir, without drawing attention. Can you move down a foot or two, and a bit to your left? Please."

"You said the magic word, 'please.'"

Woody suppressed the urge to show his excitement. "Hey, I know you—you're Joe Falooka, one of the top boxing contenders a few years back."

"How did you end up here?" said Joe, fumbling with the key chain.

"They're about to release the world's deadliest bacteria, and watch me die for their own amusement. Would you be so kind as to get me out of here? Please? Sir!?!"

"I appreciate a young man with good manners." Joe tried one key after another on the first key chain.

"Don't leave me here!"

"Wait, I've got some more keys," said Joe.

"When that red light starts flashing, there are going to be about a billion germs let loose in here. Hurry up, please, please, pretty pretty please!"

"I've got it!" Joe unlocked the door, and carefully opened it.

"Wait a sec," said Woody. "They've got me on camera but I don't think they can hear me. Can you switch off that box? And the camera?"

"Sure thing."

The red light on the black box started to flash. Joe quickly turned it off, and pulled the plug on the camera.

Woody was so relieved his eyes watered, and he sobbed. "Thank you, thank you, Mr. Falooka, kind sir." Joe quickly slashed off the restraints with his Bowie knife.

"And for you, Mr. Falooka, sir, I have a thank you gift. I believe it's called a failsafe device, and I can show you where they moved it and a shortcut to get there."

Luciano, Enrico, Mario and Lucia shivered in the near freezing temperature. Mario's hands were shaking as he loaded a grenade launcher, and he pinched one finger in the mechanism, emitting a loud *OOOWWW!*

"Quiet you meathead!" Lucia whispered, smacking him on the ear. "Them guys can hear you from here."

No one in the family noticed an extra light come on in the Hip Hop boys' barracks.

Lou and Tanya followed Mei step for step through the blackness of the château's basement, going more on instinct and the soft patter of her feet than any visual clues. The sound of a few buttons being pushed was followed by a rush of warmer, stale air from somewhere above. Mei took Lou's hand, he took Tanya's, and in a daisy chain they crept up a worn, stone staircase.

Many steps later, they arrived at a landing. Mei pulled the trio closer and whispered in the dark. "As soon as I open this door, we must keep absolute silence. It will be pitch black, so hold my hand and follow me, through the chapel, across the hall, and into the library. Then it should only take a couple of minutes to set off the failsafe device."

Tanya stopped them and whispered "Shoes off."

Mei slowly opened the door to more blackness, and a slight breeze of fresher air. In stocking feet they emerged into the chapel and tiptoed, step by step. Both Lou and Tanya had their pistols ready, safety mechanisms off.

A few more steps to the door and Mei squeezed Lou's hand to stop them. She gently pulled Lou's shoulder around the doorframe, and pointed down the hall to their right, where a streak of light could barely be seen, scarcely illuminating their faces. Lou mouthed the word *Library?* and she shook her head. She mouthed the words *Professor Pfizz's study* and did a little mime of Erik in his wheelchair, smoking a joint, and an up and down hand motion, a silent masterpiece of uninhibited mugging. She crept a few steps further, and listened, her hand cupped to her ear. She looked back at Lou and imitated someone snoring with her mouth wide open. Lou mouthed the words, "Someone may still be awake," pointed to his wide open eyes, and pointed his gun in the direction of the study.

Inch by inch they crept down the hall on deep piled carpet. The snoring grew louder as they drew closer to the study, and Lou could distinguish three or perhaps four different snores.

The first thing Lou saw in the dim light was a blank TV screen, then four dozing figures in the front row of the small lecture hall, with no weapons in sight. Karl was nearest the door. Lou pointed to Karl and then to himself, and gestured to Mei to stay back. Tanya took a solid position braced against the doorway, ready to take out DeWang, Atlas and Erik in less than a second.

Lou silently approached the would-be saviour of the planet and said, "Happy Earth Day, Karl," as he pressed his pistol under Karl's chin, pointing the barrel toward the brain stem. Karl's eyelids slowly peeled open.

The interior door to Erik's quarters flew off its hinges and Joe leapt through the shattered frame, a pistol in his hand. Woody cautiously followed. Erik, Atlas and DeWang awoke with the noise and instantly realized the game was over.

"Joe, search them for weapons while Tanya and I cover them," said Lou, not taking his eyes or his pistol away from Karl until Joe had finished. Only then did Lou relax a little and step back a pace.

"Luigi Gubriace, at last we meet," said Karl, with a hint of a smile.

"Call me Lou, please."

Mei stepped into the doorway, with a brilliant smile that felt ten miles wide.

"Mei, my little vindictive Valkyrie of vengeance. My heart soars like a giant condor whenever I see you."

"Where's your little *cowgirl* friend, Karl? And as for you, I hardly recognized you without your *towel!*"

An uncomfortable silence ensued, which Woody finally broke. "Aha, here it is, under about a pound of dope." He gently slid the failsafe device from Erik's desk, and said, "I think Lou should do the honours." He carefully set the device on the edge of the desk nearest Lou.

The sounds of gunfire and grenades exploding rattled the windows slightly. Mei looked at Lou and said, "That would be the sound of the Hip Hop boys being woken up in the morning, Lou. Our team of *real* professionals can keep them at bay easily."

Lou checked that Joe and Tanya had the room covered, and picked up the failsafe device. The red *READY* light was flashing.

Karl smiled his most sincere smile at Lou, and the words oozed out like honey from the honeycomb. "Go ahead Lou, push the buttons if you want to. I'm sure Mei has told you the code."

Lou looked the device over carefully, examining the keypad, the display screen, and the switch which would put it into *STANDBY* mode. Then he locked eyes with Karl.

"I can feel what you are feeling, Lou. I've picked up on some of your thoughts, and I've had those thoughts too. You know as well as I that the world is in terrible, terrible trouble. You know the one crucial problem that cannot be solved by conventional means is overpopulation, and that it requires a radical solution. Did you ever say to yourself something like 'I would give anything for a real solution'? Lou, listen, listen carefully, please, for just a minute. We are *all* doomed if nothing is done. You know that. This is not about killing 6.8 billion people who you very well know are as good as dead already, and who will suffer much more cruel and agonizingly slow deaths from starvation or war than the easy death which follows a few hours of coughing. It's all up to you now, Lou, you can *save* the lives of more than a billion people, billions of animals and countless other species, and create a new world, a true renaissance, where humanity can finally live in harmony with nature."

Tanya kept her pistol trained on Karl's head. "Do not listen this, Lou, he knows your weaknesses—he is Satan."

Mei hissed, "Lou, I warned you he's been engineered to make himself the most charming and convincing creep on earth. He can't possibly be right. For crying out loud, stop playing Hamlet for once in your life and just push the buttons and blow the whole shebang up, will you?"

A sparkle in the eye and a gleam of a perfect smile, and Karl said, "Somewhere in the deepest, darkest corner of your mind, in your heart of hearts, you know I am right."

Lou turned the switch to STANDBY, and pointed his pistol at Karl. "No, Karl, it's not because you have convinced me of anything, and you haven't thought of anything that is not obvious to me. I must compliment you on your charming *snake oil* salesman routine—it's quite an act. It's not because in most people's minds the prospect of killing billions of people is unthinkable, and that you and I can see that as a possibility. It's because, because, . . . it's just because."

Lou tossed the now disarmed failsafe device to Karl. He turned to Tanya and whispered one last, "Sorry," put the muzzle of his pistol into his mouth, and pulled the trigger.

As some of Lou's mortal remains spattered onto the TV screen and dripped down, like streaks of spaghetti sauce with ground beef and porcini mushrooms, a platoon of Hip Hop boys burst into the room from both doorways, guns blazing.

The floor director of the ECO TV studio in Paris counted down from five and gave the *go* cue.

"Good evening, everyone, and what a week it's been since Earth Day," said Neville Lear in his *bad news* voice. "The epidemics, which had been erupting in isolated locations for some weeks previously, finally broke out around the globe. After what has felt like a hellish eternity, finally at noon today authorities from the Mendel Foundation confirmed that the plagues have indeed burned themselves out, and the worst death toll the world has ever known is now over. ECO TV reporter Solange Du Morgue attempted to interview a senior Mendel scientific advisor today.

A video insert showed Erik racing as fast as his wheelchair would go toward the Mendel Foundation building, with Atlas jogging alongside. Solange shouted, "Professor Pfizz, Professor Pfizz, the death toll from the plagues is now confirmed at 7.2 billion people dead. Can you give our viewers a comment for ECO TV News?"

Erik stopped his wheelchair as Atlas opened the door for him, turned to Solange and said, "OOPS!" and scooted into the building.

Neville turned to the camera. "'OOPS.' That's all, just 'OOPS.' We're not entirely sure what he meant by that." Neville shook his head and shuffled his papers.

"Other scientists, including Dr. Karl Mendel himself, wish to reassure the survivors that the epidemics are clearly a naturally occurring event, a result of wanton destruction of the rainforests and the release of new organisms into the world.

"Despite the horrendous loss of life, and the political and economic chaos that will likely continue for some weeks or even months, there is some good news to report. Atmospheric scientists state that for the first time in decades, the average global temperature has begun to decline slightly, and air pollution has already dropped to a level not seen since the mid 20th century. Most amazing of all, armed conflicts and criminal violence all over the globe seem to have entirely ceased, as areas with active combatants and high criminal activity seem to have been afflicted by the epidemics much more severely than others. *Hmmm.* No one left to start a fight, I suppose. And miraculously, key centres of industry, commerce, education and agriculture all around the globe are almost completely unaffected."

He paused and stroked his chin, stared into space, and mumbled, "Bad guys dead, good guys OK. *Hmmm.* How about that? Amazing. *Hmmmph!*"

Neville set aside his papers, faced the camera directly, and returned to his professionally sculpted voice. "I guess there's always a silver lining to any cloud, and, who knows, maybe in the long run we survivors will all be better off. As my grandmother, Bambi 'Bubba' Lear, used to say: *Never fear, never worry, Mother Nature always finds a way to save the day.*"

AFTERWORD

In case anyone suspects that there is a real conspiracy brewing to rub out billions of people, allow me to reassure you that *The Telomere Conspiracy* is a simple satirical environmental story, inspired by a myriad of conspiracy theories on the internet and other media. A recent Google search with the key words *overpopulation, conspiracy, environment* returned over 2,000,000 results. Entertaining and risible as such conspiracy theories may be, I doubt that any such conspiracy exists, and conclude that the only entity that might eliminate billions of us in the coming decades is Mother Nature.

According to the best sources I can find, creating a telomere-like structure to limit the reproductive capabilities of deadly bacteria, as vaguely described in the story, is a biological impossibility. If I am wrong, it would be moderately perturbing to learn that I have inspired the worst terrorist device in history.

Lou's concern for the environment, with overpopulation being "the hard problem," is a reflection of some serious thought by some very fine minds (see below) and a satirical tale struck me as a way to nudge the conversation from a state of denial to one of anger, or maybe even bargaining about how many people would constitute a reasonable number of earthlings.

What do you think? What will happen in the future of those who are now young adults? Are we headed to mass annihilation in the near future? Will we pin our hopes on someone thinking of something eventually? Do you hate thinking about these things?

You are welcome to share your thoughts via an e-mail to:

thetelomereconspiracy@gmail.com

I have a policy of responding to any e-mails that are both short and interesting.

For those who are interested in population and the environment, and for those who would like to know more about our hero, here are some of Lou Gubrious's favourite books and other things, in no particular order:

The Vanishing Face of Gaia, James Lovelock, 2009
The Population Bomb, Paul Ehrlich, 1968
The Limits to Growth, Donella H. Meadows, et al, 1972
An Inconvenient Truth, Al Gore, 2006
Peak Everything, Richard Heinberg, 2007,
The End, Scientific American, Sept 2010, [special issue]
Lou's favourite movie: *Dr. Strangelove*, a satire on the cold war
Lou's favourite bathroom reading: *The Living Planet Report*, WWF, 2010

Lou's favourite BBC doc: ***How Many People Can Live on Planet Earth?*** 2009

Lou's favourite websites: ***prb.org*** and ***albartlett.org***

Lou's favourite overpopulation essayist: ***Isaac Asimov***

Lou's favourite form of exercise: aerobic fretting.

Finally, a few thank you's to some very special people.

This story was originally conceived as a movie, and I am grateful to Nika Rylski and George Higton for their generosity of time and insights on the screenplay version.

I am fortunate to have had a number of readers who kindly read a draft of the novel and provided some very helpful feedback, including Joanna Yao, Virginia Reh, Holly Bowen, Ian Werker, and George Pawlak. Apologies for any names omitted.

A trio of very patient editors slogged through a rough draft, correcting innumerable errors and inconsistencies. They are the most admirable Jack McCaffrey, the eagle-eyed Patricia Tomlinson (who also torqued and tweaked the computer files) and the curmudgeonly but crafty Lorne Hicks.

I also wish to thank the staff of *iUniverse* for their most courteous and professional help, without which you would not be reading these words.

Any remaining errors and ludicrous ideas are, of course, my own responsibility.

"OOPS!"

Bruce Mason
Toronto, Ontario, Canada
October 31, 2011.